Merry & Happy Tamara
Love + Sparkles
Nancy LeHmon
(now one of the Bake Shop Girls!)
xo
Nancy

"Remember it's the simple things in life that are the most important!"
Isabella xo

Isabella
Reunites the Healing Faeries

Illustrated by

Arden Belfry and Nancy Lee Amos

authorHOUSE®

AuthorHouse™
1663 Liberty Drive, Suite 200
Bloomington, IN 47403
www.authorhouse.com
Phone: 1-800-839-8640

© 2008 Nancy Lee Amos. All rights reserved.

No part of this book may be reproduced, stored in a retrieval system, or transmitted by any means without the written permission of the author.

First published by AuthorHouse 11/14/2008

ISBN: 978-1-4343-9310-4 (sc)

Cover and Isabella designed by Arden Belfry

Printed in the United States of America
Bloomington, Indiana

This book is printed on acid-free paper.

CONTENTS

PART I: Isabella on the shores of Prince Edward Island 1

PART II: Isabella in France 27

PART III: Isabella Returns to Scotland 55

The Meaning Of The Words
'Believing In Miracles' 73

The Healing Faery Creed 74

Epilogue 75

Wee Pictures from Author's Own Scrapbook 77

Sample Pictures of Actual "Faery" Special Gardens/Creating and Using
your Faery Healing Gardens 105

The Healing Faeries Seven favorite herbs/plants/oils and their healing properties 133

The Healing Faeries Seven favorite Healing Stones and their healing properties 137

Dedication and Tribute to
Lucy Maud Montgomery 143

About the Author 154

Notes for Faery Faith Friends, Special birthdays, Faery sightings and Magical moments/blank pages 163

Dear Peoplefolk: Throughout this story the spelling of the word 'Fairy' has been changed to 'Faery' as requested by the Faeryfolk!

****

- A Scottish Faery Tale -

For all you Lads and Lassies
All over the world
This story is for you
It's all about believing
In dreams that do come true
This is the *'second'* story of Princess Isabella
Caught *between two worlds*
She takes you on a quest
Will she stay a *faery* – or become a *folk* like you?
For Princess Isabella, this will be a test
So catch a cloud of *faery dust*
It's not to late to start
It's what the faeries live for
It's the greatest part of *all*
It's not too late to answer, the *Healing Faeries* call!

****

ISABELLA
The Princess of the Healing Faeries

Isabella on P.E.I.

Lupine Flowers of P.E.I.

Isabella in Scotland

French Lavender

Scottish Pine

Isabella in France

This book is dedicated to all those who *'Believe in Miracles'*

and the *'Miracle of HEALING'*...

****

'Tis time for the *healing* of the world
And the healing in each one of us
Believe in Isabella and the *HEALING* faeries do
And know till this day they still walk among us
Guiding us with gentle steps
Sprinkling us with 'miracles and gifts'
Right in *front of you!*

It's really quite simple – *all you have to do*
Is LOOK UP! LOOK UP!
Your *miracles* – are right in front of you!
They're in this present moment, on this precious earth
You only have to take this time before this day is through
To count the many *miracles*, <u>*right in front of you!*</u>

Sprinkles of love and faery dust...

ISABELLA, 'Princess of the Healing Faeries'

-Isabella on the shores of Prince Edward Island-

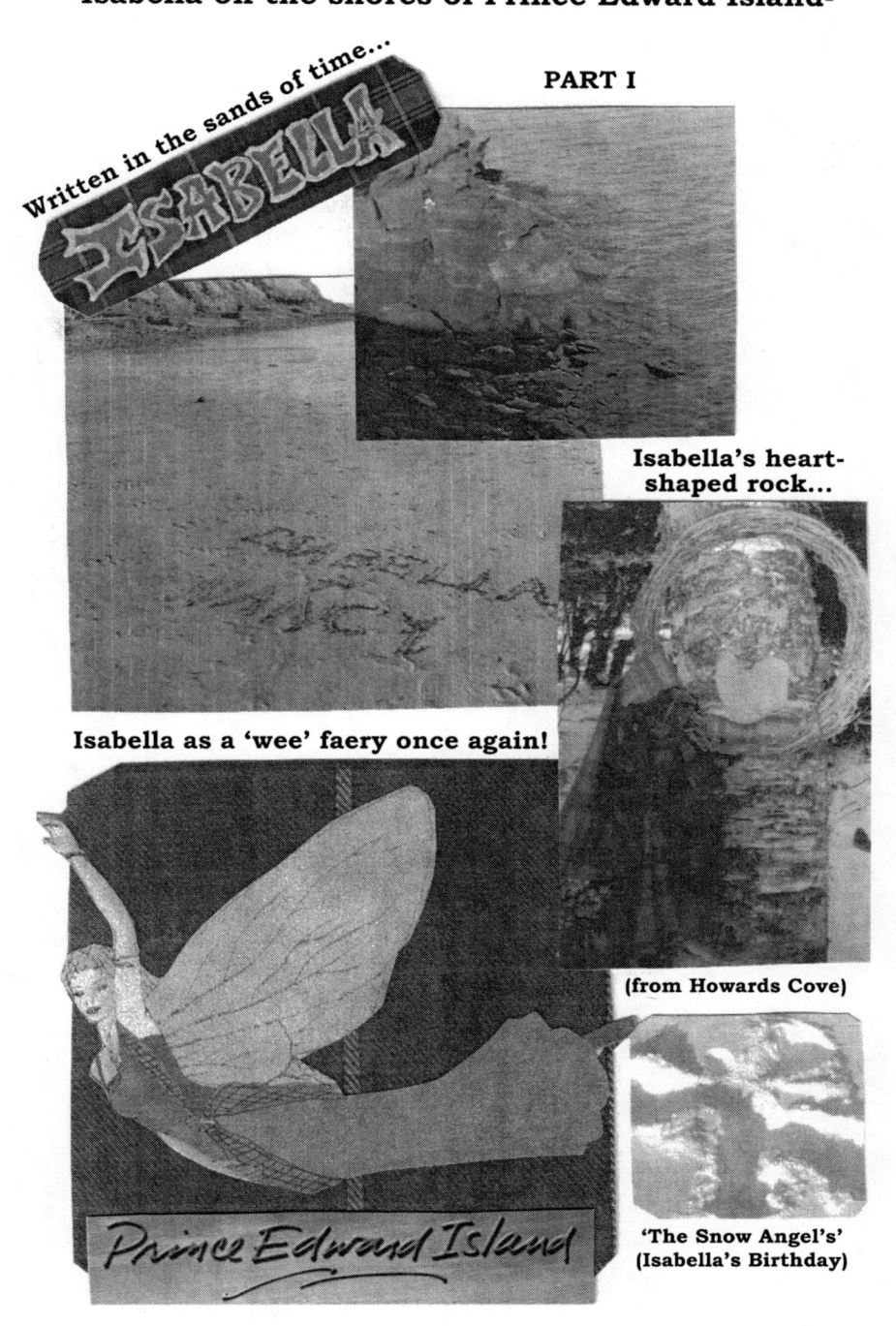

Written in the sands of time...

ISABELLA

PART I

Isabella's heart-shaped rock...

Isabella as a 'wee' faery once again!

(from Howards Cove)

Prince Edward Island

'The Snow Angel's' (Isabella's Birthday)

PART I

Autumn had arrived – the air was cool and crisp, with no wind; the magical colors of the leaves *sparkled* in the sunlight as Isabella breathed in the familiar *smells* of the ocean and the red earth all around her! The Princess was excited as she stood on the edge of the woods waiting for Gabriel and her father; this was the day she would become a *wee* faery once again and she was ready! Isabella quickly turned as she heard the crunching of leaves behind her! There stood her father, tall and proud holding her tartan scarf in his hands; Gabriel arriving only seconds behind as he struggled to keep up with the King's *youthful* strides!

"Here Lass, you may need this; 'tis cool this morning!" he said as he gently wrapped it around her shoulders. Isabella draped the fabric over her shoulders quickly securing it around her waist.

Isabella's azure blue eyes were brimming with excitement; her long curly hair hung loosely framing her tanned face. She had waited all summer for this day! Gabriel was still out of breath as he stood smiling down at Isabella... Today he would become a *Healing Faery* and today Isabella would *fly* by his side!

"Ok Laddie and Lassie, are ye ready?" her father bellowed. His smile was as wide and broad as Isabella's.

"Aye, we're ready!" said Isabella looking over at her cousin. Gabriel stood waiting proudly wearing his grandfather's *Scottish key* around his neck.

As soon as the King spoke a few words in Gaelic blessing them both – things began to change. First they both became *smaller* and then in a flash they disappeared. Within seconds they reappeared as *wee* faeries! Gabriel was *amazed* – all he remembered was hearing these words over and over...

> Spinning, Spinning... round and round
> Taller, taller... Smaller, smaller
> Spinning your web, weaving your dream
> Let your magical *wings* be seen...

Gabriel looked down at his *gossamer wings* fluttering to and fro - he could *fly*! "Be off with you then!" said the King quickly brushing a tear from his eye. He had done his duty teaching Gabriel the laws and creeds of the Healing Faeries; now it was up to Isabella to show him the life of the *faery realm*. He knew how much the Princess needed to heal. Enough time had passed and Isabella felt safe; *now* she could feel the joy of being a 'wee faery' once again!

"Gabriel, let's go to the faery ring!" cried Isabella. As they flew off disappearing into the bright sunny morning Gabriel's dog Sandy chased them all the way into the woods barking and frolicking with them! Higher and higher they flew darting in among the pine trees finally coming to rest on a sturdy pine bough. Both were excited as they sat for a moment trying to catch their breath!

"I wish my grandfather could see me now," said Gabriel proudly.

"And your mother!" cried Isabella.

"Was my mother ever a wee faery Isabella?" he asked.

"Aye," said Isabella. "I saw her once at our wee faery castle in Scotland; she was very beautiful! I heard she liked to stay with mother and father at the big castle," she added.

Gabriel then became quiet and Isabella could sense he was thinking of his mother. "Come, I'll race you to the faery ring!" yelled Isabella flying off ahead of him. Not long into the woods Isabella stopped in flight, her faery senses tingling; they were not alone! The air sparkled with faery dust and mischief. As she darted around for a closer look she found Martha, Tom and Sara sitting atop some mushrooms! Some of the Healing Faeries had come to join in their celebration.

Martha was Isabella's favorite Healing Faery! She reminded her so much of Nanny Belle. They and about seventy-five of the Healing Clan had followed King Roy and Queen Eve to the Island more than four years ago and Isabella knew each and everyone of them!

"Hello my dears!" cried Martha.

"You made it Gabriel!" Tom said joyfully. "We knew ye would lad!" he added. Isabella and Gabriel flew down to join them.

"Look, I'm the size of this mushroom," said Gabriel laughing happily.

Isabella

"Aye," said Isabella. "And if your dog finds ye, you'll be his food!" she replied. They all laughed.

"Come, my friends," Sara said excitedly. "We have a surprise for you! The King made us promise not to show you till today."

"Follow us!" they cried.

As Gabriel and Isabella followed them to a grassy knoll Isabella stared in disbelief! There before them was a faery mound, the castle entrance hidden by a small bush. "Come inside!" cried Tom. "'Tis time to celebrate..." he added, his voice filled with merriment.

Inside, the castle was decorated with tiny furniture made of willow and ash. On the table, among the small plates of fruits and vegetables sat a jug and five goblets filled with daisy wine. "A table fit for a King!" cried Gabriel.

"A table fit for our Princess!" Tom said as he bowed before Isabella. He then brought out his tin whistle and started to play the most beautiful music. As Gabriel and Isabella started to dance around the table Sara and Martha joined in. Gabriel had never seen Isabella as happy as she was that day. Together they had laughed and danced and sang till the wee hours of the morning.

Finally bidding a 'goodnight' the others left leaving Isabella and Gabriel alone; they had everything they needed. Isabella could tell her mother had done most of the decorating; each room was almost identical to the 'wee castle' in Scotland.

Isabella was so grateful to her parents. As she walked around touching everything, Gabriel followed her in utter amazement! In every room you could smell the *hint* of lavender, one of the clan's favorite healing herbs! Isabella recognized some of her mother's *small treasures* from Scotland and the Healing Clans' plaid colors were everywhere. It was a 'luxury haven' for little people! Isabella felt so loved and blessed! It was so *healing* for her to feel this life once more; it felt so much like Scotland - so much like 'home'.

It was a full harvest moon that night and in a couple of hours it would be daylight. Isabella and Gabriel decided to go down by the water where they sat side by side on the sand. Gabriel sat there thinking of the first time they had met; it was on the very shore where they sat right now, but this time it was different – this time they were *wee faeries*!

"Gabriel," said Isabella slowly. "There's something I have to do. You may not want to come, but..." she stopped as Gabriel reached for her hand.

"I know what you're going to ask," he said. "And the answer is, *yes*!" he replied quickly.

"You'd go to France with me to find your mother?" asked Isabella, excitement rising within her.

"Yes, now I'm *ready*!" he replied bravely. "I'm so grateful to you and your family! You helped me become a *Healing Faery* and now - its time to find my own family!" he added.

Isabella was silent as she sat thinking of her own plans. It was time to reunite the Healing Faeries, starting with *Gabriel* and *his mother*! Isabella would go to *France* – then to her beloved Scotland. Seeing the first hints of sunrise they flew back to the castle on the grassy knoll. They each found a comfy bed and off to sleep they went.

Isabella awoke first around mid morning feeling refreshed and content – not tired at all. The Princess quickly got dressed wearing a pretty new blue-green gauze dress; tying her thick hair back with a silver clip - she went to find her family. She wanted to talk to them about her plans as soon as possible.

Isabella flew to the garden first where she found her mother working. Isabella perched on the gate, watching her. The Queen was still a very beautiful woman; each time she bent over, her long red braid would almost sweep the ground. The Princess was so happy she began to sing; the sweet sound of her voice filling the morning air like a songbird. Her mother turned around giving her a bright smile. "Lassie, my *wee faery*, you've come back! Did you like your surprise?" she asked.

"Oh mother, it was a heavenly surprise! I had no idea you'd done that for us," cried Isabella.

"There was plenty of helping hands from the Healing Faeries! And it was your fathers' idea to try to make it identical to our castle in Scotland," her mother replied happily.

Isabella closed her eyes and changed herself back to her mothers' size; within seconds she was *without wings* - what a gift they shared!

She then went to her mother hugging her close, "I love you mother and I thank you!" whispered Isabella.

"And I you my darling daughter! And I you! Let's go inside and I'll make some rose hip tea," she said. Inside the King was waiting for them. With his keen sense of 'second sight' he knew the Princess needed to talk; he already had the water boiling for tea!

He gently hugged Isabella good morning. Taking her face in his hands, he asked, "Now, what did you want to talk to your mother and I about Lass?"

"Father – now what makes you ask that?" asked Isabella smiling up at him.

"Well, I see travel in your eyes; am I right? Your mother and I thought perhaps France would be the place!" he added with a grin.

Nancy Lee Amos

"Oh father, I can never hide anything from you!" she cried. "I want to find Gabriel's mother Emilie, your sister and Gabriel wants to come with me!" she added hastily.

Anxiously her mother looked up at the King. "Isabella, we know you have to go – but can't you wait till spring?" her mother asked.

"*We will wait till spring; with plenty of time to say 'goodbye'*!" chirped in a *wee* voice. They all turned to see Gabriel *sitting* on Isabella's teacup! They all began to laugh.

After tea and more 'laughter' they spent the rest of the day in the garden; together they gathered seeds, herbs and fall vegetables for the winter.

That night Isabella and Gabriel went back to the castle. Tom had a fire going for them. The King had decided to make Martha, Tom and Sara caretakers of the *wee* castle, they loved the thought of looking after Isabella and Gabriel for the King and Queen for the winter!

Gabriel would still help her father with the chores and get to use his 'new powers' everyday. Isabella and her mother were kept busy preparing bundles of herbs and supplies for the villagers for the winter. Her father and the Healing Faeries were busy making furniture out of willow and ash. The King did not shy away from taking part in the daily living of his people.

Quickly winter settled in around them, the castle was so alive with the younger ones inside. Tom loved watching them dance to his music and loved telling them story after story about life in Scotland in the 'good old days'; Martha loved cooking for them and Sara loved their company.

It was coming onto December and close to Isabella's *birthday*. Gabriel and Martha had been scheming for days. They'd overheard Isabella telling her mother she wished she could go on a sleigh ride and they knew one of the villagers who had a sleigh. Tom and Gabriel had a plan; they would *surprise* her! It had snowed a lot in the last few days and would be perfect for a sleigh ride!

On the night of her birthday Isabella had dressed up warm and went out to find Gabriel. The snow had stopped and it was perfect for making *snow angels*. Isabella found that with their powers they could go from faery size to peoplefolk size in the 'blink of an eye'!

Nancy Lee Amos

The Princess knew Gabriel had been busy all day with her father so he must not be far. Tonight was her birthday and she was feeling *lighthearted* and *free*! She had waited all day to let loose and play. Although Isabella was sixteen years old, she still had a playful spirit and *loved* the snow. She had decided to make seven snow angels, as *seven* was the Healing Clans favorite number! When Gabriel came around the corner - he found Isabella lying in the snow.

"Isabella, what are you doing?" cried Gabriel.

"Making *snow angels*!" Issy said excitedly as she moved her arms and legs to and fro. "Every time you make a snow angel – you set them *free*!" she added breathlessly. "Come on Gabe, make some too!" she urged.

"Who can say *no* to you Issy?" Gabriel laughed, as he lay down in the snow beside her. Only *visible* to Isabella's eyes were the snow angels already twinkling and spinning as they danced above their heads. Isabella was in her glory as she started singing her favorite *winter* healing song!

> *Winter splendor* at my feet
> Knocking at my door
> Set me free to dance with you
> Let me spend another day

Covering all in sight
With my *mystic* white
Of *'heavens perfect snow'*
Winter splendor at my feet
Give me flight oh silent night
To sparkle, shimmer and delight
To be your *'angels of the snow'*
To sparkle, shimmer and delight
In *perfect full moon's* glow
Let me free to dance and play
Until I have to go...

This is how her father and Tom found them... There stood Gabriel and Isabella covered in snow with at least *seven* snow angels at their feet! The full moon was starting to come out *lighting up* the figures in the snow. "Look Tom," laughed the King, "it's an army of snow angels guiding us tonight!"

"Aye and I think we could use them now!" said Tom cheerfully signaling Gabriel it was *time*.

Just behind the barn was a 'different' scene! A crowd had gathered with at least twenty villagers and their children and just as many of the Healing Clan. In front of them stood a large wooden sleigh decorated with pine bows and holly led by two spirited horses – their sleigh bells jingling as they waited to be on their way! Majestically the King had made 'small wooden candleholders' and placed them in the snow to spell out *Isabella's* name; the candles like the excitement flickered and danced in the December air!

After much laughing and frolicking in the snow Gabriel had finally gotten Isabella to follow him... Before they even made it around the corner of the barn everyone started yelling excitedly, "Surprise! Surprise, Isabella!" Isabella stopped in her tracks! With all the powers she pocessed the Princess was totally spellbound by the scene before her! She had no idea... All at once the people started gathering around her wishing her a 'Happy Birthday'!

Isabella was half-laughing half-crying as she was *lifted* up into the sleigh. Quickly, the others joined her. As the horses led the sleigh down the hill Isabella looked up at the six people gathered around her - Gabriel, her parents and her three closest friends. One by one as the lamp flickered and lit up their rosy faces Isabella was overcome with emotion. The night sparkled with love, faery dust and a magical time she would remember forever!

Isabella closed her eyes and thought, "Everything is in this present moment, everything is *right here, right now*! If I could teach *one thing* to all people it would be to just 'look up' and see the magic in the *now* - the sky, the trees, the people and the beauty surrounding them. *This is how you create – heaven on earth!*"

Just as Isabella opened her eyes Tom began playing a familiar tune – the *song* of the Healing Faeries, a song they knew well. They called it, 'Believing in Miracles'. The Healing Faeries believe that *anything* is possible – but *only* if you *truly* believe! They also believe that you are the maker of your own dreams and the only one who can *spin them alive*!

The sleigh ride ended that night on the steps of her fathers' home. The house had been decorated with pine bows, holly and lots of candles. A big fire was blazing in the old stone fireplace. Fresh hot apple cider and daisy wine sat waiting. The table was laden with food; *everyone* was welcome!

Isabella was now sixteen years old and a beautiful young woman. For the Healing Clan, their Princess was now at the age to become Queen. That night she was given many gifts; homemade preserves, scarves, shawls, aprons - all made with *love*! Her mother and father gave her a beautiful mirror and brush set! They were silver with a green 'oriental design' *hand painted* on the back. They had been given to her mother as a *gift* from the peoplefolk

Queen of Scotland and her mother had saved them for Isabella!

It took Isabella many hours to fall asleep that night; it was a night she would always remember! Seeing the Healing Clan and the peoplefolk together made her long to see it in Scotland once again. Together they had danced and played their music; together they had eaten and drank at the same table! The Princess knew it was her destiny to find this *peace* once again in Scotland and she was *ready*.

The winter months flew by and soon the grass was sticking up through the snow. You could watch as the warm sun melted the snow right before your eyes. *Spring* was coming to Prince Edward Island and Gabriel and Isabella knew what this meant; it would soon be time to leave - but not *today*... This was one of those special times when *miracles* were about to happen. It was one of those spring mornings when the birds were all out singing, the blue jays and chickadees were lined up in the trees, the robins out searching for worms for their young.

That morning, Martha had come out to dump ashes from the fire and there in front of her eyes were four Flower

Faeries dancing in front of the castle door! Martha ran to get Tom and Isabella.

"Tom, Isabella, come quickly!" cried Martha.

"What is it Martha?" asked Tom.

"The Flower Faeries are here!" exclaimed Martha.

Isabella and Tom followed her to the door. There on the path in front of the castle were four flowers and no *faeries* to be seen! Tom was not familiar with the Flower Faeries so he asked Isabella, "What do you think Lass?"

"Aye, it's the Flower Faeries!" she said excitedly.

"Only Flower Faeries can disguise themselves that fast right before your eyes," Martha whispered knowingly. Isabella finally coaxed them to 'come out' as *Flower Faeries* using daisy wine and fresh milk! Isabella hadn't seen Flower Faeries since leaving Scotland and there before her eyes were *four crocus faeries*!

The first crocus faery spoke softly in a *wee* voice, "We were afraid to come out. We watched you become small, with wings and without!"

Nancy Lee Amos

"Yes," added the second crocus faery, "we didn't know what creatures you were!" Isabella eased their fears by demonstrating her powers.

"You see Flower Faeries, we will not harm you – we are the Healing Faeries!" said Isabella as she quoted them a poem from the Healing Clan book; one of her favorites!

> We are the Healing Faeries
> We are the ones that sing
> We believe in *freedom*
> No harm to anyone
> We may be small we may stay tall
> We may just *disappear*
> But when you need us most – just know
> That we are always near
> We're like the wind, the earth, the sea
> Just like the skies above
> You will *sense* that we *are there*
> For you will *feel the love...*

Isabella didn't stop there; she told the Flower Faeries all about Scotland and how it used to be. That spring the Flower Faeries became *regulars* at the wee castle everyday, *that spring*, the Healing Faeries had the 'best gardens' they had ever seen. Everyone worked together digging and planting, watering and watching their harvest grow. When the sun turned warm and everything turned green Isabella knew it was 'time' to go!

Isabella

Their *secret* faery realm had grown and the faeries had a safe haven to go whenever they wanted, the castle was open to them all. The King and the Queen had plenty of help and many new friends. The King and Queen were also ready to give up their titles to the young and soon Isabella would become Queen. It was written in the sands of time and in their trustworthy *clan's* book! It was time to say goodbye...

Isabella and her mother walked along the beach together one last time! The Queen knew they would see each other again, but not on this shore! It was a typical Island day, sunny and warm with a slight breeze. Isabella and her mother both had their hair tied back in *braids* – something they always did when walking by the shore. Hand in hand they walked along – so much to say, so little time. Eve knew her daughter was leaving – she had to be brave. Just like the night they left Isabella in Scotland; that was one of the hardest things they had ever done and now, Isabella had to do the same.

Her mother gathered up their seashells and the *heart-shaped* rock Isabella had found and started up the hill. Once again – it was time to pack!

"Mother," said Isabella as she took her mothers arm in hers, "I want you to know I'm ready to leave - I can always come back, in a *blink of an eye*!"

"Aye, my brave Lass, you can," her mother said gently. "You have all the powers you need to stay out of trouble and then some!" the Queen added lightheartedly.

"And I won't be alone; Gabriel will be with me!" said Isabella, reassuring her mother.

"Ah...speaking of Gabriel; he's staying pretty close to your father these days," said her mother.

"Aye, he will miss him as much as I," said Isabella softly. Just ahead they saw Gabriel and the King on the front veranda sitting side by side in the willow and ash chairs, it was then that Isabella began to cry...

Later that day her father helped Gabriel pack for his journey giving him instructions who to contact when they arrived in France.

Gabriel took plenty of food and his lucky horseshoe his grandfather had given him. The King had given him a clan plaid blanket as a gift and together they rolled all his belongings into it. Earlier that morning Isabella and Gabriel had said their good-byes to Tom, Martha and Sara; now they felt ready to go!

Isabella was finding it difficult to pack; once again she had to leave some things behind. On the shelf she left her doll on the wooden horse and her basket of faded flowers from Scotland. She packed her mirror and brush set, some of her rocks, shells and some dried Island flowers. In her sewing basket she packed her smaller *treasures*, as Nanny Belle used to call them. Looking around the room Isabella's thoughts went to Nanny Belle and William; soon she would see them again. As she held William's poem against her heart she whispered, "My dear William – soon no distance will ever come between us again!"

Finally Isabella wrapped one of her most favorite possessions, her *heart-shaped rock* from the shores of Prince Edward Island. It was on these shores that Isabella found peace, freedom and much love. It is here that she shall leave her *heart*!

Gabriel and her mother were waiting for her in the kitchen. Her mother noticed Isabella still wore the amethyst necklace and bracelet she had given her; like her Scottish braided key, she never took it off. They were apart of her. The Princess had become a 'gifted healer' while on these shores; her mother had taught her the healing ways of the *herbs* and the power of the *crystal stones* and everyone knew Isabella had a *powerful gift* to share.

Now, it was time to go! King Roy and Queen Eve walked Isabella and Gabriel down to the cliff overlooking the cove. Gabriel felt a bit nervous, but as he watched the Princess she was smiling at him. He remembered how she had mystically arrived on these shores not so long ago and she had made it *just fine*!

The King stood in front of Gabriel, his long gray hair, his *trademark*, blowing in the wind. Standing tall and proud he handed Gabriel a small velvet covered book. "Take this book and treasure it!" he said. "'Tis mine, I have no use for it anymore – I know it off by heart," he added with a jolly laugh. The King grabbed Gabriel and gave him a rough hug and wished him luck!

The Queen hugged her daughter close as she started to cry. "I promised not to cry!" she whispered.

Isabella

"It's alright mother," said Isabella softly. "I'm off to *reunite* the Healing Faeries!" she replied bravely, trying to smile. "I'm Princess Isabella - the *bravest* Lass of all and I'm going to miss you *both*," she added her voice faltering as she pulled her mother and father to her!

The next moment they heard the dog barking, circling around them. "Sandy!" cried Gabriel. "You can't come girl," he added more gently.

"Why not?" asked Isabella as she continued, "Father if Gabriel could hold her, could she come?"

"Well..." said the King hesitating, "you would have to hold both your bags Issy!" he added quickly.

"Then it's settled then!" said Isabella in her stubborn tone; the *one she used* when there was no changing her mind! Gabriel let out a big smile as the King helped him get ready... As Gabriel sat with the dog in his arms, Isabella did one last thing.

Before picking up their bags she grabbed some of the *bright red earth* stuffing it into her cloak pockets. Just as the sun reached the cliff, Gabriel, Sandy and Isabella disappeared!

-Isabella in France-

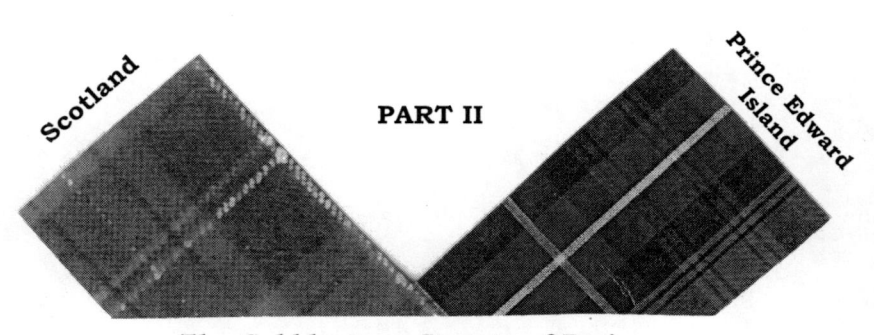

PART II

Scotland

Prince Edward Island

The Cobblestone Streets of Paris...

The Inn
'Le Parrot'

The Lavender Fields

PART II

The King and Queen stood on the cliff overlooking the ocean. The Princess was gone. The King was not one to show his emotions but as he stood there that day, tears stinging his eyes, he wondered if he would ever see his daughter *set foot* on the shores of Prince Edward Island again! In the haste of saying good-bye the Queen had almost forgotten to give Isabella a braided lock of her hair; a *'sign'* the Healing Faeries gave you to let you know they would see you again.

Isabella and Gabriel were now on their way to France; their lives woven like the *plaid tartans* they wore everyday, the *threads* of their dreams intertwined. They were ready to heed the 'call' of the Healing Faeries and this is what they heard...

>Spin your dream as though with thread
>Spinning, spinning round your head
>Chanting and spinning
>Spinning and chanting
>Round and round ye go

Nancy Lee Amos

The next thing Gabriel heard was the sound of Isabella's voice. "Are you alright Gabriel?" whispered Isabella. Gabriel opened his eyes and looked up. He was sitting on the ground still clutching the dog.

"I think so!" Gabriel said slowly.

Before he could say another word Isabella suddenly grabbed his arm. "Quick Gabe, get up from the road! There's a wagon coming!" cried Isabella. Swiftly Gabriel pulled himself and the dog to safety. They just had enough time to look up and see the end of a beautiful black carriage race down the cobblestone street, the sound echoing against the stonewalls! It came so close they could *smell* the horses as they passed and *feel* the *wind* against their faces!

Isabella and Gabriel looked around trying to get used to the darkness; a single lamppost on the corner was their only form of light. "Where are we?" asked Gabriel.

"It's Paris!" cried Isabella. "Look! That's the great city wall father told me about. Let's hurry!" she added.

"Wait Issy lets disappear so we can look around more easily!" said Gabriel excitedly.

"Good idea," replied Isabella, "one, two, three!"

As they both turned around they're sat the dog head to one side looking for them! "I think I need more practice!" said Gabriel, stifling a laugh. Reappearing Gabriel took hold of the dog; this time the dog *vanished* along with him.

As Gabriel followed Isabella through the wide stone archway into the city they both were in awe at the sight before them. Not far from the gates were rows of buildings and shops; the streets filled with people *boisterous* and *loud* speaking in their native French language. Although no one could see them Gabriel and Isabella could see one another. Not long into the city Isabella motioned Gabriel to follow her into an alley; garbage was strewn everywhere, the smell, intense! Quickly they became *visible* again moving back out into the dimly lit cobblestone streets. Isabella stopped as she bravely peered up into her cousin's dark blue eyes; adjusting her tartan, standing proudly she said, "Let the *quest* begin!"

The first thing Isabella and Gabriel had to do was find the Inn called 'Le Parrot'. But Isabella and Gabriel were not prepared for what they saw in France. Being able to walk around freely as peoplefolk was not always a 'good' thing... While some people were shouting and dancing in the streets others were begging for food and money with outstretched hands!

Isabella came to a woman who was walking down the street towards them. "Excuse me," said Isabella. The woman stopped and gazed at Isabella, "we are looking for an Inn called Le Parrot. Can you help us?" continued Isabella – not sure if the woman understood her or not.

"Ah, but you are standing right in front of it Ma Cherie!" she replied.

"Oh, thank you!" said Isabella kindly, nodding to the woman. As she looked up at the tall wooden structure Isabella could not help but wonder how her father could know anyone in *Paris*, especially the Innkeeper and his daughter!

The first thing that caught her eye was the bright hand painted sign hanging above the door; it was *shaped* like a parrot! As they weaved their way up the crowded steps they reached the door to the Inn. Everyone stood aside staring at them as they entered; perhaps it was the clothes they wore, their tartans draped across their shoulders or the telltale signs of 'newcomers' with their belongings on their backs!

"Come in! Come in!" the people shouted motioning with their hands to join them. The newcomers made a handsome couple; Isabella's beauty was astounding and Gabriel's chiseled features were unassuming!

But Isabella was mesmerized herself as she moved through the crowd captivated by the music coming from the front of the room. The music, together with the girls' voice was the most beautiful thing she had ever heard!

Gabriel left Isabella for a moment as he made his way over to the man standing behind the desk; he asked him if he knew of a man named Pierre. "I am Pierre!" shouted the man in a jovial manner. "And that is my daughter, playing the harp!" The tall rugged man held out his hand to Gabriel. "What is your name lad?" he asked.

"My name is Gabriel!" shouted Gabriel above the crowd.

"Ah, I've been expecting you!" said Pierre brightly. "King Roy sent word you were coming!" he added.

Gabriel started to relax as he listened to the friendly man's voice – liking him already! "That must be Isabella, non?" he asked not waiting for an answer. "And your partner by your side does he have a name?" he added with a wide grin.

"My dog's name is Sandy and it's a 'she'!" replied Gabriel smiling back.

"Well, she is welcome too!" he answered as he patted the dog's head. "Come, the night is still young my friend!"

That night they befriended the Innkeeper and his daughter, Cecile. The Innkeeper's daughter agreed she would help them find Emilie.

With incredible luck Cecile had a good friend Rosetta who worked for a Scottish woman in a mansion just outside the city walls. She was sure the woman's name was Emilie!

But Cecile had to warn Isabella to be careful; the mansion was totally surrounded by stonewalls and *inside* surrounded by guards!

But Isabella was not afraid; she would use every ounce of her *powers* to find Gabriel's mother if she had to!

That night Isabella slipped out into the warm Paris night, *alone*! Making sure all the others were asleep and unaware of her plans the Princess went to see Emilie *first* - before she took Gabriel!

It didn't take her long to find the place Cecile told her about. The size of the mansion and grounds were impressive even on a dark cloudy night! Using her faery powers Isabella slipped through the iron gates; once on the other side she flew into the open windows overlooking the courtyard garden. The only thing she heard was the sound of dogs barking in the distance. Once inside Isabella took her time as she went through each room admiring the beauty that surrounded her. It reminded her so much of the palace the King and the Queen of the peoplefolk lived in, in Scotland; it was uncanny!

In her *homeland* of Scotland Isabella never ventured far from the faery realm, but once, at the request of her mother, she had gone with her to the palace of the *peoplefolk* King and Queen. Their son had taken ill and they had called on her mother to help using her herbs and *healing* ways.

But no one knows to this day just how many times the Princess had gone back to visit the Prince - *on her own*! He was her first 'peoplefolk' she had ever met and Isabella knew the Prince and his family *truly* believed in her mother and the Healing Faeries!

Isabella would sneak into the palace and they would spend hours together; the Prince would take her all around the palace – dancing and playing, hiding and seeking, playing small tricks on the older housekeeper named Jenny! She knew the palace off by heart - every room, every nook and cranny! *This mansion* was no different; it was filled with plenty of *magical* places to hide...

As Isabella started up the stairs she could faintly hear someone crying; following the sound she came to the large French doors of the library - there to her surprise sat Emilie, Gabriel's mother; she was alone!

Boldly, Isabella became peoplefolk size appearing before her!

"Why are you crying?" the Princess asked softly trying not to startle her.

Isabella

Surprised Emilie straightened out her dress peering up at Isabella. "How did you get in here? Who are you – are you a new servant?" asked Emilie sternly.

Isabella came over and stood in front of her. "I'm not a servant! I am Isabella, Princess of the Healing Faeries!" she said as she pulled out her tartan scarf hidden beneath her cloak. "And you must be Emilie, my fathers sister!" she added more bravely.

"You are mistaken – I do not know you!" she said quickly. "Leave, or I will call the servants to come and get you!" she added nervously. As Emilie started to stand up, Isabella disappeared!

"Where are you – where did you go?" she cried as she turned looking in all directions. Isabella watched her from the table then flew to the mantle *appearing* before her once again. "Go away or I'll call the guards!" she cried.

"Aye, you can call them," Isabella said deliberately, "but it won't matter; I can disappear or become as small as your teacup!" she said defiantly standing before her.

"Please just go away!" Emilie pleaded.

Nancy Lee Amos

"I will not go away till you say you will see your son, Gabriel; he wants to see you!" cried Isabella.

With these words Emilie's face went ashen and white; running from the room, she called for her servants! Quickly, Isabella disappeared; Emilie was not ready to talk to her or *admit* anything! Just as Isabella flew out through the window she saw the same fancy black carriage they had seen their first night heading straight towards the mansion; Isabella hurried back to the Inn!

The next morning she went to talk to her new friend Cecile. "It doesn't look good Cecile," said Isabella sadly. "She pretended not to recognize me or believe anything I said!" she added.

But the Princess recognized Emilie; with the raven black hair and the eyes the same *deep blue* as Gabriel's – it had to be her! The only thing the Princess noticed that had changed was that her Scottish accent had *faded* with time.

Cecile touched her arm and said, "I'm sorry Isabella! My friend Rosetta says she is very beautiful, but very spoiled! Some of her gowns even have *gold thread* running through them…" she added dreamily. "They say her husband is a rich Prince from Scotland, his name is Prince Ivan!"

"Aye, that's him!" cried Isabella. "He's the man who fell in love with her and took her away from the…" Isabella stopped for a moment. She didn't want to tell Cecile the whole truth just yet. "From her family!" said Isabella finishing off her sentence.

"Oh, Ma Cherie, I almost forgot, Rosetta told me they are having a spring ball next week!" said Cecile excitedly. "Perhaps you could *sneak* in somehow – what do you think?" she asked. Isabella slyly looked up at Cecile as they both shared a 'knowing smile'. She had done it once already – why not again? Isabella went to find Gabriel to tell him about her plan.

They decided to go and sneak in – as 'wee' faeries of course! Gabriel had mixed emotions; he was excited but also a bit nervous to see his mother again after all this time.

On the night of the ball Pierre told them he would watch the dog for them. "She can keep me company while Cecile is singing and playing her harp!" laughed Pierre. He bid them goodnight and wished them luck.

Nancy Lee Amos

Just as Gabriel and Isabella were leaving the Inn Cecile started playing a song on the harp; Isabella paused just outside the door. Gabriel and Isabella *stared* at each other as they recognized the song... Cecile, the Innkeepers daughter was playing the *song* of the Healing Faeries called *'Believing in Miracles'!*

The song sounded so *magical* and *mystical* on the harp; but there was no denying it was their song! They both turned around looking back through the crowd at Cecile and Pierre. Pierre came to them pulling out his *silver braided key* from around his neck!

Now they understood how her father knew where to send them! Pierre hugged them to him as the music played on. It's a *small world* in the 'world of faery', thought Gabriel as he smiled and waved goodnight to Cecile and Pierre. Isabella clutched her necklace to her as she looked up into the night sky. It was the beginning of summer solstice and time to put out the *call* of the Healing Faeries! Tonight she needed all the strength she could gather from her amethyst stones and her 'faeryfolk friends'. It was time to *reunite* the Healing Faeries, starting with Gabriel and his mother!

Isabella

Making their way to the mansion Isabella and Gabriel *flew* in threw the windows of the ballroom; they were *invisible* to all, only the dogs stirred by the doorway.

Inside Gabriel was overwhelmed; he had never seen anything like it, ever! Rich tapestries hung from the ceilings and everything sparkled with gold!

Gabriel followed Isabella into the main dinning room. There, she pointed to his mother standing by the fireplace. Gabriel landed on the buffet so he could look at her more closely. Isabella paused by the doorway so she could see Gabriel's face *light up* as he watched his mother laughing and talking to her guests.

His mother was standing by the mantle wearing a dress the color of *lavender*, her dark raven hair piled high upon her head; she looked radiant! At that moment Prince Ivan made a toast to his beautiful wife and a toast to celebrate the spring and the coming of summer solstice! Both Gabriel and Isabella could see how happy and very much in love they were.

Gabriel watched his mother all night trying to find a time to be alone with her. Finally, when there was a lull in the dancing he saw his mother head towards the open doors leading to the *garden*; Gabriel followed her. Waiting till they were hidden from view, he appeared before her. Immediately Emilie started to cry, for she knew it was her son!

"How did you get in here – the guards, no invitation?" she asked in a dazed voice shocked by the truth of seeing her son before her.

"I flew in!" said Gabriel.

"Oh, Gabriel you cannot fly…" his mother started to reply.

"Oh yes I can!" Gabriel stated quickly as he pulled his braided key from around his neck. "It was grandfathers and now it is mine!" he added with pride trying to shed no tears. His mother started to come towards him. "No, wait, I'm not finished." added Gabriel as he continued, "It was my right to become a Healing Faery and you left me; I didn't even know about the faery realm!" His mother stood back waiting, wanting to go to him! "Mother, look at you, you are a Healing Faery surrounded with riches yet others are suffering in your midst!"

It was his mother's turn to speak, "Oh Gabriel, I never wanted the life of a *Healing Faery* – this is the life I have chosen, this is who I want to be!" replied Emilie still wanting to go to her son.

"What about *me* mother?" asked Gabriel, carefully choosing his words slowly.

"You were fine with your grandfather!" replied his mother flatly.

"Well, grandfather's *no longer with us*!" answered Gabriel barely above a whisper. That's when she ran to him, holding him to her.

Through her tears she cried, "I'm so sorry Gabriel… I will make it up to you I promise! Please forgive me!"

Knowing the ball was almost over they spent the last hour, just the two of them walking through the gardens; you could smell the fresh scent of lavender and lily of the valley throughout.

As Gabriel talked, his mother listened… He told her that King Roy and Queen Eve had found him working on his grandfather's farm and told him they would like to

Nancy Lee Amos

help him fix it up! Together they stayed with him fixing the house, the gardens and in the spring bought it from him. Gabriel said he was about to leave the Island when Isabella arrived. It was then he learnt about his *'family ties'* and his rights to become part of the *faery* realm.

After Gabriel revealed his story to his mother she was anxious to see Isabella again. Emilie was sorry for the way she had treated Isabella the first night she had came to see her. She asked Gabriel if he and Isabella could join the party and become her *honored guests*!

His mother quickly took control and asked the musicians to stay longer – there was much more to *celebrate* than spring! Gabriel quickly found Isabella; the maids had already laid out some formal clothes for them to wear!

Emilie then introduced her son and his cousin to their guests. They made a very striking couple! Isabella was dressed in a soft blue gown the color of the pale blue sky; her hair a mass of curls fell just below her waist. Gabriel was tall and handsome in his white full shirt and his dark riding pants, his blue tartan scarf tied loosely around his neck matching the color of his eyes.

Isabella

The Healing Faeries were like peoplefolk in every way – with the exception of their *extraordinary powers*! They were also known for their exceptional *beauty* and their fine chiseled features. Everyone was talking about the two new guests for the rest of the evening. The men were smitten with Isabella – the women with Gabriel!

After meeting Prince Ivan, Isabella and Gabriel were both *surprised* at how much they liked him! When the ball was over, Gabriel and Isabella met with his mother, alone.

She asked them not to mention anything about the Healing Faeries to her husband just yet; she would tell him on her own. She begged them to stay on for another few days - which they *both* agreed!

Together they went back to the Inn to tell Pierre and Cecile about their joyful reunion. The Innkeeper and his daughter were happy for them and told them to come back and visit anytime they wished.

This time, Isabella, Gabriel and his dog returned to the mansion walking through the front gates, past the guards – with an *open invitation*!

Nancy Lee Amos

That first week, Gabriel's mother showered them with many *gifts* and clothes. They rode her beautiful horses and roamed the countryside as 'peoplefolk' and as *wee* faeries. They even came across some 'Flower Faeries' *friends* that Isabella thought she would never see again, Honeysuckle Rose, Lavender Ocean and many others... The faeries had scattered in many directions during those difficult times in Scotland and in the realm of Faery and the realm of Peoplefolk Isabella was glad to discover it's a small world after all!

Also France was known for its 'fields' of lavender and Isabella was happy to see it was harvested right outside the gates of the mansion! The French people used it for many things, for oils, perfumes, washing clothes and even for their baking. Being the Healing Faeries favorite herb Isabella thought she had discovered a *faeries* 'gold mine'! Isabella and Gabriel were in their glory, both *inside* and *outside* the mansion as they roamed the fields and countryside of France. However, they met many people who were *not so fortunate*, farm dwellers living on the outskirts needing medicines and food. The Princess and Gabriel tried desperately to help them! With the cooks help they made up extra baskets of food and herbal medicines leaving them on the doorsteps for the poor.

Isabella

This was also a chance for Isabella to use the *power* of her healing 'crystals' – her healing *stones*! The *amethyst* was the Healing Faeries favorite healing stone; but for Isabella her favorites were the *clear quartz crystal* and the *rose quartz*. The *clear quartz* majestically cleanses impure thoughts and awakens ones self to the *positive energies* needed to heal. The *rose quartz* is the love gem needed to 'open ones heart' to unconditional love and the *nurturing* needed for healing. It was said if worn *near your heart* – it could fill your heart and others close to you with a *love so forgiving* and *tolerant* like that of a 'mothers' love!

Days turned into weeks and nothing more was said in regards to the Healing Faeries; Emilie still had not told Prince Ivan 'the truth'! Isabella and Gabriel had stayed on at the mansion longer than planned - they both felt there was so much more *healing* work to be done!

But one day while Isabella was passing by Emilie's bedroom, she ran into Rosetta - in her haste Isabella had forgotten to hide *her braided key* inside her gown. Rosetta noticed the key right away! "Oh, Ma Cherie!" exclaimed Rosetta. "You are a Healing Faery!"

Isabella stared at the girl in surprise! "How did you know?" she asked Rosetta instinctively putting her hand to her throat.

As the girl pulled out her *own braided key* – she pointed to Isabella's. "My family came from Scotland along time ago." said Rosetta.

Isabella then smiled at the girl feeling a *kindred spirit* in their midst. "I am Princess Isabella, Princess of the Healing Faeries!" replied Isabella, pride filling her heart!

"Oh Princess, *it is you!*" stuttered Rosetta. "There was a rumor you were in France! I am honored to meet you!" she said bowing down before Isabella. "I have heard so much about you, all the good things you are doing in Paris; like the baskets of food and the herbs being left on doorsteps all over the countryside!" she added excitedly.

"Yes, there is so much to be done, we could use all the help we can get!" said the Princess urgently.

"You can count on me!" said Rosetta, her smile radiant, as she looked up at the Princess.

Isabella

Later that day Isabella told Emilie what had happened! She also told her about the food and the herbs, not wanting to hide the truth any longer. Emilie told Isabella she could have all the herbs and food she wanted just not to expect her to help in other ways.

That night Emilie could not stop thinking about Isabella, Gabriel and Rosetta! She had no idea Rosetta was part of the Healing Clan. Just before going to bed she pulled out her own 'braided key' from its velvet box and *slowly* - put it back on!

The next day Emilie talked to Prince Ivan. They too had heard about the *miracles* that were happening outside their mansion, in the city and the countryside. They decided they would help the Healing Faeries in any way they could; s*ecretly*, of course!

Isabella was overjoyed when she heard about their plan! Gabriel was so proud of Isabella and thankful for the changes she had made in their lives. Prince Ivan asked Isabella if she would stay with them a few more months, they didn't want her to go!

Isabella already knew what her answer would be. Just that morning in the garden she had heard the 'call of the

Nancy Lee Amos

Healing Faeries' once again. It was time to *reunite* the Healing Faeries – this time in her beloved *Scotland*!

Isabella had stayed longer in France than expected but knew things would only get better now with Emilie and Prince Ivan on their side.

Her thoughts were now on the rugged coast of Scotland and what she would find waiting for her there.

Isabella decided she would stay for the next harvest of the lavender; an event they said - she would not want to miss! The Princess would also have some to take with her on her journey.

Time passed quickly and soon it was the *eve* before Isabella was to leave! Emilie went looking for Isabella and found her packing. She had so much to tell the Princess before she left. "Isabella, I don't know how to thank you for bringing Gabriel back into my life – *and for this*!" Emilie said as she pulled her *Scottish key* from around her neck. As Isabella looked up at Emilie's face she now knew the journey 'had been worth it'! "You know I can't leave France Isabella, but take this *gift* to remember me by," said Emilie softly.

Isabella

Isabella looked down at the *amber* ring Emilie had given her. "This ring is the 'symbol' for your undying loyalty and your *true healing spirit* Isabella!" said Emilie as she continued… "*Amber* has always been the stone of the 'ancient pine trees' - bestowing gifts of patience and strength for all those who wear it. It will also bring love, healing, wisdom and purity for all who come in contact with its *golden hue*." As she slipped the cool amber ring on Isabella's finger she added. "You will make a perfect Queen for our people my dear sweet Isabella!"

That night they had a private gathering at the mansion for Isabella. All the Healing Faeries throughout the countryside were invited. It was a celebration like no other in all of France! You could be whoever you wanted to be that night. All who worked for the Prince and Emilie were faithful to the *secret* of the Healing Faeries!

Many surprises awaited Isabella that night. When Gabriel had left Prince Edward Island, Tom and the King had hidden a gift of a 'tin whistle' inside his bag! For months Tom had been teaching Gabriel to play - so that night Cecile and Gabriel played the *song* of the Healing Faeries for their Princess. With Cecile's mystical harp and Gabriel's Scottish tin whistle there wasn't a dry eye in the room! They knew that soon Isabella would become Queen and many of the Healing Faeries were ready to follow her back to Scotland.

It was hard saying good-bye the next day; but with their *extraordinary powers* they knew they could travel back and forth in the faery realm to see one another! Gabriel told Isabella he had decided to stay in France! He had grown fond of the Innkeepers daughter *Cecile* and together they would stay and help the people of France.

Gabriel would never forget what the Princess had done for him and his mother – *reuniting them* once again! Gabriel, along with his dog Sandy were welcomed everywhere with open arms! The faeries were akin to all animals and Gabriel was so grateful to have his dog with him!

Isabella had no regrets about coming to France. The Princess now understood what Emilie saw in the peoplefolk way of life! Isabella knew she could use her faery powers in many ways to be closer to the faeryfolk and the peoplefolk she had come to love.

After many good-byes the only *ones* Isabella wanted by her side were Gabriel and his dog Sandy! As they stood outside the city walls Isabella spoke to Gabriel, "When things settle I want you and Cecile to come visit me in Scotland! Perhaps one day, your mother will come too," she added as she stared up at Gabriel taking in the features of his face, etching it into her memory. The two cousins had formed a *faery faith bond* on this journey to France; one, many people would never reach in a 'lifetime of togetherness'.

Gabriel helped Isabella lift her heavy bundle from the ground. "Thank you *precious* Isabella! You will make a wonderful Queen for our people!" he said bending down to hug her. Isabella kissed and hugged him one last time as she secured her leather straps holding her belongings.

Bending down she kissed the dogs head. Looking back she gazed back at Gabriel, "Till we meet again my cousin!"

Isabella took a deep breath – she was ready! As she stood on the dusty road that day, her eyes closed, the Princess knew every tingle, every shiver and every word of the Healing Faery chant off by heart... In *seconds* she was gone!

-Isabella Returns to Scotland-

PART III

QUEEN ISABELLA!

Scotland

The rugged coast...

Isabella's Crests

PART III

Isabella did not know what to expect as she appeared on her beloved *coast of Scotland* that night... As the Princess opened her eyes, she could feel the cool damp air. She could smell the sea and feel the mist on her skin. At that moment Isabella was overcome with joy and the 'sheer magic' of being a Healing Faery traveling through the *faery realm* as she did now.

It was dark, but she could still see the outline of Nanny Belle's cottage in the distance... Isabella hurried towards the old stonewall. As she got closer her *faery senses* began to tingle but not in a *good* way; she could feel something was wrong! When she got to the gate she saw the front door of the cottage ajar, swinging in the wind!

Isabella's strength began to waver. As she sat her heavy bundle on the ground all sorts of thoughts ran through her head. Gathering up all her faery strength she knew she could not give up now. She ran to the cottage first but it was completely empty, nothing but a shell. Next she ran to the barn where her horse Gladiator used to

Nancy Lee Amos

be. Standing in the doorway of the barn her heart ached for some kind of sign from Nanny Belle and William, any sign that they were near. There was *none*!

Isabella had to keep going! It was late fall and it was getting colder, the days shorter. The winds had picked up and the cold went right through her. She undid her bundle getting out her heavier velvet cloak to put on. To lighten her load the Princess left her belongings hidden in the barn. She knew where she had to go next! Using her special powers she became the size of faeryfolk and *flew* to the faery mound where their *wee faery castle* used to be. When she arrived she found it in ruins, just a pile of rubble; the ground surrounding it rocky and barren. Isabella flew to one of her favorite places not far from the ruins, an old Scottish pine tree. At least some things would never change she thought! As Isabella took in the *fresh smell* of the pine she remembered what Nanny Belle used to say. The smell of pine was used to 'refresh your spirit' making you feel *alive* and *full* of healing energy!

It was then that the Princess *remembered* her *own* saying, "All you have to do is look up – *look up* and see the miracles surrounding you!" At that moment while Isabella was staring up into the dark cloudy sky an opening came in the clouds and some stars appeared. Instantly she saw a *falling star*! It disappeared quickly – falling in the direction of the road where her father and mother's large castle was. It was a sign! She had to go there right away! Feelings of hope started to dwell inside Isabella as she quickly flew in the direction of the *falling star*. As she arrived by the castle walls the Princess shivered. She remembered standing in that same spot just four years earlier with her horse Gladiator and her dog Wallace.

Suddenly it started snowing the heavy thick snowflakes accumulating fast; the wind gathered speed as it *whipped* the snow and her long tendrils of hair across her face! The Princess quickly lifted up her hood pulling it tightly around her face. As she looked up she thought she saw lights *flickering* through the gates across the courtyard! The Princess knew the snow could be playing tricks on her, but she knew there was only one way to find out!

Isabella knew if the castle was truly identical in every way to the 'wee castle' there was a secret passageway to get into the courtyard! She had to see who was inside her father's castle! Knowing she could easily fly through the gate it may be easier to be peoplefolk size to get into the

Nancy Lee Amos

castle. As she made her way towards the entrance she thought she heard a dog barking in the distance.

Isabella tore through the old tangled vines finding the cold metal latch of the door. Once again Isabella heard a dog barking but closer this time. It was snowing so hard the wind and the snow took her breath away. Inside she staggered towards the sound of the dog!

All of a sudden she saw the dog racing towards her and she whispered hoarsely, "No, it can't be!" Even through the snow she could see it was *Wallace*. He was so excited; he knew it was Isabella. She fell to the ground holding the dog to her, crying softly, "Wallace, my Wallace!" The Princess was so busy hugging the dog that she didn't notice William standing in the courtyard watching her!

After a few moments William called the dog to him using his *old familiar whistle.* Isabella turned slowly not even noticing the cold or the snow any more. She was so glad to hear that familiar whistle and to hear that familiar voice. Isabella tried to get up and run in the direction of William's voice, but stumbled to the ground. William grabbed Isabella as she fell into his arms. She tried to speak and ask where Nanny Belle was but she was too exhausted. Her words were lost in the wind. "Shh, its

Isabella

ok Lass come inside where it's warm!" William said his Scottish brogue so comforting to Isabella's ears.

Isabella hardly remembered much about that first night... Nanny Belle had gotten her into a nice warm bed; they had stoked the fire and let her sleep - they were so happy to know their Princess was home and that she was *safe*!

The next morning Isabella woke to see Nanny Belle by her side. It was a *reunion* she would never forget. Isabella wanted to get up and see everything; she wanted to see William, the castle, she wanted to see it all but Nanny Belle wouldn't hear of it! Even in her tiredness she still had the spunk and spirit of the 'old Isabella' but because of her experiences she had *wisdom* beyond her years. Nanny Belle could tell she had turned into a *beautiful young woman.*

Over the next few days there was lots of excitement and flurry of activity inside the castle walls! Isabella was back to her 'old self' and nothing could keep her down. She was amazed how the castle was identical in everyway to the *wee castle* where she used to live before it was destroyed. Isabella wished her mother could see their castle was safe, well cared for and *filled with life*!

Nancy Lee Amos

Later that day Isabella got to talk with William alone in the small library off the main hall. William told her what had happened after they had left. They waited weeks before things settled down enough to get back inside the castle. The peoplefolk had finally left and they all gathered together to repair the damage that was done.

As they sat and had tea by the warm cozy fireplace William continued; he seemed excited to share more with her. "With lots of love and care the castle has become a *haven* for our people, the wee folk and for those who choose to be the size of peoplefolk like us!" he said cheerfully.

"Oh, William I don't know how to thank you; there's plenty of room for us all!" cried Isabella knowing this was one of her hopes and dreams for her people.

"Come, my Princess I have a surprise for you!" said William as he guided Isabella to one of the rooms they called, 'Heaven on Earth' for the *wee faeryfolk*. As they walked down the long corridor they came to a room closed off by two large wooden doors – the doors were *etched* with beautiful 'carvings' of flowers and high above were two small openings left 'open' for the *comings and goings* of the wee faeries!

Isabella

Inside, the room was full of plants and vines and little houses all colors, shapes and sizes! In the middle of the room was a huge rock and on that rock sat *Isabella's dollhouse*! William told her he had gotten the idea when she had left it behind! The Princess was overjoyed as she stood with her hands against her lips, just looking at everything. There were birds flying freely overhead high in the domed ceiling and some of the Healing Faeries had even come out to greet her, welcoming her back home!

The Princess was filled *with love* for all that William and Nanny Belle had done while she was gone! The castle had become a safe haven for all and a place of *freedom* - the *symbol* for the Healing Faeries!

That night Nanny Belle went to Isabella's room to look at the 'small treasures' she had brought – *memories* of the last four years! It was such a *miracle* for them to be together once again. Isabella showed her the 'heart-shaped rock' from Prince Edward Island and told her how *precious and healing* the Island had been for her. The Princess was also filled with *gratitude* for the time she had spent with her mother and father there, a time she would never have again. Isabella had gained so much wisdom and knowledge from being in their presence and they had lovingly shared the many wonderful 'faery faith friends' they had with her. Issy was also excited to tell Nanny Belle all about the teachings of the 'healing crystals' and show her the stones, her *amber ring* and tell her of their meanings! There was so much to tell...

"Oh, Nan, I am so glad to know you are a *Healing Faery* – if only I would have known back then – I was such a *retched faery child*!" she said her voice *begging* for forgiveness!

"Oh no Lass, you were a *joy* in our lives at such a trying time! I am so proud of you and all you have done! You did it Lass, you did it!" she cried as she grabbed Isabella off the bed making her dance around with her till they were both *dizzy with delirium.*

Isabella also got to share the 'bounty' of the *lavender* with Nan. The Princess now knew how to travel back and forth in the faery realm to get more if needed, there was plenty more where that came from - not to mention how to *visit* dear friends! It was the start of winter now and they had plenty of time to prepare for spring – the time when their Princess would become *Queen*! In the 'Realm of Faery' it was the Queen who chose her King

Isabella

and Nanny Belle was happy to know that the Princess had chosen *William*!

The months flew by quickly for Nanny Belle, William and the Princess. The winter was filled with laugher, love and lots of 'Healing Faeries'! There was plenty of music, dancing and frolicking and of course *not to mention* Isabella's *birthday*! The Princess was the only one they knew who liked to start celebrating her birthday the first day of December, making it last 'till months end'! Nanny Belle had the wedding all planned; the gardens arranged and all the final details - *in her head*! She was thrilled to have the Princess at home and in the company of her own people! William and the Healing Clan were kept busy making lots of willow and ash furniture for the *extra* guests that would arrive in the spring! Like her *father*, William did not shy away from working along side *his people*!

The Princess was busy herself – but not with the *'wedding'* plans! She had gone to see Prince Davey, her peoplefolk friend; this time Isabella arrived at their door the 'same size as peoplefolk' – *without wings*! The King and Queen and Prince Davey were so surprised and happy to see her; they found her beauty *breathtaking*. She was greeted with 'open arms' for they were so grateful for her mother's help so many years ago! They were pleased to find out Gabriel and his mother were reunited and thankful for the news of their son, Prince Ivan! It was certainly a time for *celebration*!

While the Prince had taken Isabella on a tour of the changes made to the castle, the King and Queen had made a promise to one another! To *repay* Isabella and the Healing Faeries and as a 'gift' for Isabella becoming Queen they were going to give Isabella's clan *land* all along the *eastern coast of Scotland*!

The Queen had another *gift* for Isabella – her own token of appreciation, a *rare shaped* jade necklace! She knew how much the healing stones meant to the Healing Faeries - this one would be used to bring their worlds together. The Queen had traveled to many distant lands when a child and had heard about the many teachings of stones, herbs and had seen some *miracle* healings herself! She knew Isabella would appreciate the 'value' of the gift! The Queen was a wise woman who knew this stone was sacred and an omen of balance and peace, mixing tranquility with wisdom, uniting *matters of the world* with *matters of the heart*!

Isabella's destiny was close to being fulfilled, her greatest *dreams* coming true! This was a new beginning for the Princess and her people. To be given land where 'the sun rises above the sea' and with each new sunrise; *faith and hope* are born!

The Princess was sent home that day in one of the Kings *finest* carriages lead by six white horses. It was a gift given as a *pact* between the King and Isabella. She could 'ride like the wind' or 'fly like the wind' but the pact was - to *rule like the wind*. For now, only the King and the Princess of the Healing Faeries knew what this meant! The King sent one of his men to follow Isabella bringing back the horse she had came there on, her *precious* Gladiator! It was a sight to behold as the Princess rode in through the castle gates that day! The news of the *lands* spread like wildfire!

With the *arrival of spring* the final pieces of Isabella's destiny were about to unfold! Everyday people came from far and wide. The Princess was totally surrounded by family and friends, peoplefolk and faeryfolk alike. Isabella's mother and father came with many of their *faery faith* followers and friends from Prince Edward Island. Her mother also had brought with her Isabella's *doll on a wooden horse* and the 'small treasures' she had left behind! She also had a special gift for her; a lock of her favorite stallion's hair, the horse she loved on Prince Edward Island. This token was given as a 'gift' for you to know you will see them again; a fact her mother knew for sure!

Then at last - the *surprise* arrival of Emilie, Prince Ivan, Cecile and Gabriel from France made Isabella's world complete! It took longer for Emilie and Prince Ivan to arrive by ship, but they had made it! *No one* wanted to miss out on this celebration!

Isabella's mother came to her the morning of her wedding - the day she also would become *Queen*! "My darling Isabella – we have watched you grow from a *wee faery* into a beautiful young woman!" Eve said as she hugged her daughter close. "'Tis a proud day for your father and I."

"But mother…" Isabella cried out nervously. "I'm afraid!" she added as she pulled her wrap tightly around her.

"Afraid?" asked her mother. "*My* Isabella…afraid?" she laughed.

Isabella

Isabella couldn't help but smile. "Oh mother, I'm afraid I can never be *like you!*" Isabella blurted out.

Her mother cupped her daughters face in her hands looking straight into her eyes and said, "YOU are my *brave heart*, Lass! Go out there and stand before your friends and loved ones – always remembering this rule; never reign a 'step above anyone – always one step below' always reigning *side by side* and you will be the perfect Queen!" Eve, without a backward glance departed quickly leaving her daughter alone.

She could still hear her mother's voice out in the hall busily giving orders to the servants as she gazed at her reflection in the mirror! The Princess squared her shoulders taking in a *deep breath*; a mass feeling of calm filled her soul as she finished preparing for the *most important day of her life*!

As Isabella fussed one more time over her hair she glanced down at her dresser as she laid her brush down. There on her dresser was a 'button' - a *button* from her fathers' cloak! Leave it to her father not to come see her but leave her his 'sign'! Isabella held it to her then quickly got her dear friend Rosetta to sew it onto her sleeve; the joke will be on her father when she shows him! Oh yes,

Nancy Lee Amos

Rosetta was there to share this day with her; this was the one day Isabella would cherish forever! This was a *once in a lifetime* celebration where she would be totally surrounded with family and friends *under one roof*!

The ceremonies were held at the *Castle Heatheren* on the 6th day, the 6th month, the season of *new beginnings*! It was truly a wedding of 'healing hearts' and a crowning of a 'promise of peace'! Together William and Isabella planned to rule their land with love and gentle ways!

As Isabella watched from her throne that day she thought maybe it was time to start a *new chapter* in the Healing Clan book or perhaps even a *new book*! For this was the beginning of a *new freedom* for the Healing Faeries where there were no divisions and no hiding of anything - they had their land, their laws and *they were free*. It was the first time in history where the *large* Kingdom and the *small* Kingdom were *united as one,* at last!

The End

The Crowning

*

CONTINUED ON NEXT PAGE…

Isabella

WELCOME QUEEN ISABELLA TO HER THRONE

As *Queen Isabella* stood up to greet her people that day she was a sight to behold; although dressed in the 'finest of gowns' she wore the blue tartan of the Healing Clan draped across her shoulder and the tartan of Prince Edward Island tied about her waist! She would always remain *true to herself* and *her spirit* but Isabella would never forget those who helped her along the way! Isabella had her favorite stones in a leather pouch tied to her waist, within it the healing red earth of Prince Edward Island mixed with her Scottish soil! To Isabella it was the 'perfect healing blend'!

Standing by her side was William who never once stopped *believing* in Isabella – always knowing she would come back to them. For in his pocket was Isabella's poem, a *cloth* filled with *lavender - along* with a 'lock of her hair'; a sign the Healing Faeries left to let you know *they would return...*

> **"No matter how long,**
> **No matter how far –**
> **Never give up on your dreams!"**

Nancy and Isabella, *Queen* **of the Healing Faeries**

Scotland

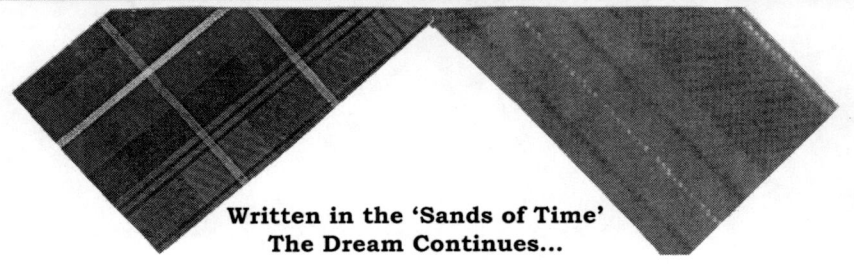

**Written in the 'Sands of Time'
The Dream Continues...**

Isabella

THE MEANING OF THE WORDS:
(*Also name of the Healing Faeries song!)
'BELIEVING IN MIRACLES'

B   - Be
E   - Extremely
L   - Loving
I   - In
E   - Every
V   - Visible and
I   - Invisible deed
N   - Naturally
G   - Giving

I   - Inner
N   - Nourishment

M   - Mending
I   - Impossible bridges
R   - Radiating
A   - Acts of
C   - Compassion
L   - Laughter
E   - Expressing life and
S   - Selfless love

THE FAERY CREED

FOR THE HEALING FAERIES

Till Heaven above and the Earth we love are as one –
We will never leave you
The Faeryfolk believe everything you will ever need
Is in this <u>very moment</u>...
EMBRACE it – cherish it and respect it.
With each new sunrise you have the chance to begin again!

The Healing Faeries also believe we still have time
<u>To heal our Mother Earth</u>...
Each one of us before this day is through
Do something to help save our 'Heaven on Earth'
Walk more, drive less, pick up litter or plant another tree
We can make a difference for our children – just do it and see
The TIME IS NOW – THE PLACE IS EARTH – LOVE IT TO LIFE!

'Create her rebirth'...

Isabella, Queen of the Healing Faeries

****

EPILOGUE

"Oh how we wish things would always stay 'the way they are'...*Forever*!"

In *our world* things are constantly changing and in Isabella's *new life*, hers was <u>no different</u>! For just *two years* later something *unforeseen* happens! The 'King of the peoplefolk' suddenly dies leaving the safety and the peaceful existence of The Healing Clan balancing in a sea of danger! Although his son Prince Ivan can take over the throne...*he does not want to be KING*! This leaves only his brother. Although young and not as *experienced* as his older brother Prince Davey tries to make a stand against the rebellion but is overrun before he can ever become King. The Prince goes to fight beside Queen Isabella and King William's side; his mother, the Queen of the peoplefolk flees to France, leaving all she has behind!

Now *it's time* for Isabella to *heed the words* of the King - you can 'run like the wind' or you can 'ride like the wind' but the *pact* is to *RULE LIKE THE WIND*! In Book III in *the last* of the Isabella series you will come full circle living your life through the 'eyes' of Isabella and bringing *all you have learnt* into existence while learning the *greatest lesson of all!* How far will *you go* to make your dream come true and who are the ones who will be left *standing with you* in *the end*? Join Isabella in her last heroic effort to *make her dream come true*!

PRINCE EDWARD ISLAND

SCOTLAND

'A Wee Bit of Pictures'

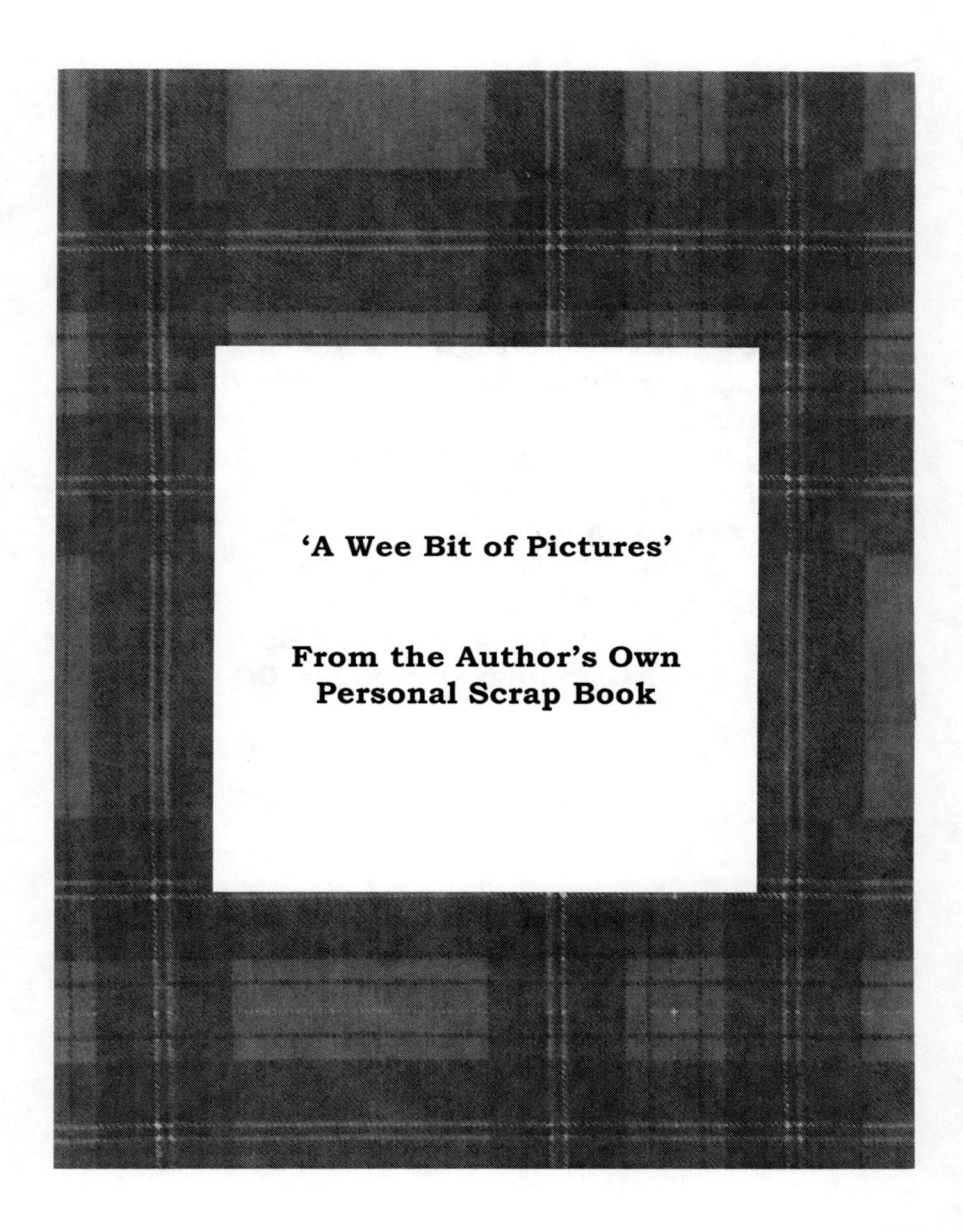

**From the Author's Own
Personal Scrap Book**

AUTHOR'S NOTE

'The making of this Second Book
 Is nothing short of bringing us *closer together*
 Weaving our lives like *the threads of a woven tartan*
 Remembering only what's *IMPORTANT*
 'THE *SIMPLE* THINGS IN LIFE'
 Friends, family, a touch, a hug,
 A small 'gift' from a *friend*'...
 'Keeping the Fairy Faith is SIMPLE'...
 All you have to do is BELIEVE'!
 All you have to do is...*DO IT <u>NOW</u>*!

In the Faery Realm there is no tomorrow...
 <u>everything</u> is in the NOW!

Before I start...My Poem to you!

'Gifts'

Gifts are treasures
Given by *friends*
Treasures are *hugs*
So our *hearts* can mend'
Friends are *rare jewels*
We must *treasure for life*
Life is a gift
To treasure *forever*
So let us give *life*
To the 'things that matter'
These are the *treasures*
That make our *hearts sing*
These are the *gifts*
That the faeries can bring
So open yourselves *to receive*
Night and *day*
Open your hearts
And BELIEVE right away!

By Nancy

Nancy and her two longtime 'faery faith friends', (Kindred Spirits) on Prince Edward Island June 06' book launch!

'Beginning of Scrapbook Pictures'

*Authors Desk update - you will like these

*Book Launch on P.E.I.

*How it all began...

*Artifacts from book

Update/Move to Perth, Ontario

right up to present ...

ENJOY.......

Authors Desk – Isabella Book II

The author's desk, her cat Wallace who has watched, sat on and assisted in the whole process of writing her books! Nothing gets by his watchful eye; he is a true Faery Faith Friend of the Healing Faeries! *Then* we brought home sweet 'wee' Bella…

As you will see both fight for the chance to be in the (silver bowl) and assist with the 'goings on' of my Isabella writings! But Wallace is the oldest and does get first dibs on the best seat in house, for now…NOTE: *(Wallace and Bella were both named following the first Isabella book…However the oldest CAT does act like a dog? and wee Bella CAT sure acts like a spoiled wee 'little faery girl' fluttering all over the place but both are pure elemental DELIGHTS!)

CAKE-PARTY–CELEBRATING...
On the shores of Prince Edward Island!

*An awesome surprise from my sister for Book Launch party!

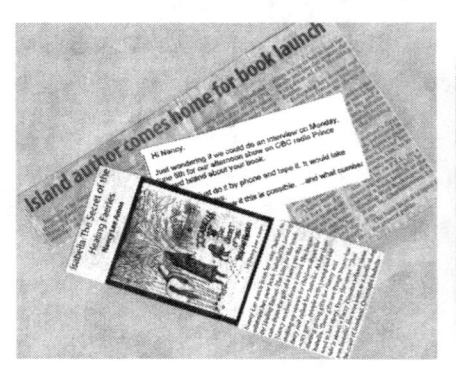

The Link...

BOOK LAUNCH P.E.I. at The Reading Well bookstore, June 2006

Above: Author standing in front of bookstore in downtown Charlottetown. Top right: Author and a 'wee friend' whose name is ISABELLA! She came to buy her *own* copy of Isabella book, poster and bookmark; her mom had been waiting for my book since *her birth*! Story *touched us all*!

Above: The author doing her presentation... left display table with artifacts from her story Right: Two special helpers, her husband and a *dear friend* who's been there since beginning! *She is still waiting for her pay cheque! xo

Above: The author with talented Island artist Arden Belfry who designed Isabella and her two Isabella book covers! Right: Author signing books for her *mother* and a *friend*! (*author wears a P.E.I. tartan skirt adorned with ribbons and Scottish pins) Above storefront a blue plaid skirt/Isabella's clan's plaid/both homemade for occasion!)

Author visits the property and family where she used to live! (*The author was a Nanny for the two English boys; she lived in a loft apartment above their home!) This is the property where they created the famous Healing Faery Circle garden!

Above: The author poses with family and neighbors children who frequented the 'faery garden' as well!
Right: The author touches the 'wee' Faery castle that is still in the garden! *She has been gone for three years and still the garden looks the same!

The author sprinkles some *faery dust sparkles* around the faery circle she had made with this family and to her 'faery faith surprise' the boys excitedly came out with a box full of memorabilia from their cherished times together!

The author was <u>very touched</u> and knew then as she left a copy of her Isabella book at the Charlottetown library there was much more to this tale than meets the eye! *Some say 'oh boys do not believe in Faeries' but I beg to differ', like my husband they see the *magic and the joy* it brings!

To this day while I was away these children have continued to *frequent the garden* and continue to celebrate its 'sacredness' giving them hope and something to believe in that will stay with them for along long time! – <u>Top left photo</u>: Garden, 2006. <u>Next photos</u>: The garden 2007; a young visitor, a friend sprinkles *faery dust* around our garden continuing the 'faery faith', *circle* of friendship and love... *Thank you for this and for the pictures!*

HOW IT ALL BEGAN...A *gift* of a Faery Pin!

ABOVE TOP LEFT: This is my journal photo album of my journey Top left: My friend who gave me the *gift* of the faery pin that started the whole Isabella story going. Top right: The cover of my first Isabella book. Bottom left: The intertwined plaids/P.E.I. tartan plaid and Isabella's blue Scottish plaid adorn a wreath in our famous faery circle garden! Bottom right: The *actual* faery pin.

ABOVE RIGHT: The author in her 'famous apron' she wore as a Nanny and will see in recent photos! As a Nanny - Nancy used to put little trinkets/treasures in her pockets for the children and take them out making up stories about them...After getting this intriguing gift of a *faery pin* she immediately started calling the faery Isabella and as the stories grew around Isabella people young and old started giving Nancy 'gifts' for Isabella and herself! With these 'gifts' Nancy creatively and magically (with the help of the HEALING FAERIES of course) incorporated them *into her story* creating a Scottish faery tale and a large following so *special* people all over wanted her book!

*THE AUTHOR IS *INSPIRED* to spin her dream alive!

The author was inspired to enter the Island's Literary Awards in the Lucy Maud Montgomery's children's award category winning an honorable mention for her Isabella. With her *following* growing and (her *big* move to Ontario) she was invited to put her BOOK not yet published on display at the Healing Arts Show located at the Charlottetown Confederation Center of the Arts; (Curator, Trisha Clarkin) Creatively in 'clothesline fashion' author displays her book on recycled paper *adorned with wildflower petals* and displays her artifacts for her story!

THE INSPIRATION – where does it come from?

The reason I am sharing all this with you is - during my Journey of Isabella I have talked with several people and they too have had dreams of; writing a book, learning to paint, a musician wanting to create their own CD or have just had an idea they wanted to share! There is a poem that I came across that has always inspired me; sadly *author UNKNOWN* - quoting just the last line... *"If you want something bad enough to work day and night for it – to fret and lose sleep over it – to eat, breathe and think of it - then by goodness YOU WILL GET IT!"*

These words have stuck with me all through this journey whenever I would get discouraged! I also believe like the Healing Faeries that with each new day, with each new SUNRISE we have an opportunity to begin again; to completely start over, create a new project or *finish* an old one! The one main ingredient I find for me is *DETERMINATION*! Each *day* force yourself to do ONE THING towards your goal and by goodness it FAERY WELL will *HAPPEN*! On the following page you will see pictures that have stuck in my mind for many years – places, drawings, ideas surfacing when least expected which *added* to my dream!

BELOW TOP: Now gone, this *beautiful fun sign* on our P.E.I. highway was for the park called FAIRYLAND! Each day I would drive by, imagination *spinning* watching the white haired man in the pumpkin coach with the six white horses; all these years stuck in my mind, buried, but *never forgotten* – now getting to use this vision *partially* in my book! BELOW LEFT: This packet of Scottish heather seeds were lovingly given to me by a dear friend who lived in SCOTLAND (and now) P.E.I. – this 'gift' was from her own *treasure chest*! She also has given me many Scottish treasures as well for wedding gifts and *JUST BECAUSE* gifts ever since this book! I will treasure them all, *thank you*! BELOW RIGHT: Last but not least this is my own first drawing depicting my Isabella *cover*... *All these things* build upon your dream; this is what DREAMS ARE MADE OF! Things that have inspired you – people who have influenced you and helped to shape the person who you have become! These are the 'makings for dreams'...

Artifacts from Isabella books!

Isabella's 'wee' sewing basket, her mother's silver mirror, her green barrette (sitting atop the sewing basket), lace from her mother's dress hangs from inside the basket, lavender and Scottish thistle, the heart-shaped rock from Howard's Cove

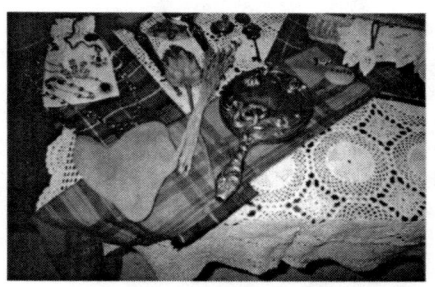

You can see a closer look at the rose embossed silver mirror, the heart-shaped rock, to the left you can see the silver chain of Isabella's amethyst necklace and bracelet <u>BELOW</u>: The tartan scarves /Isabella's blue tartan and the Islands brownish/red and green tartan! Last picture to the right you can see the magical/Scottish *key of freedom* from the book in the middle and the oriental and silver mirror set

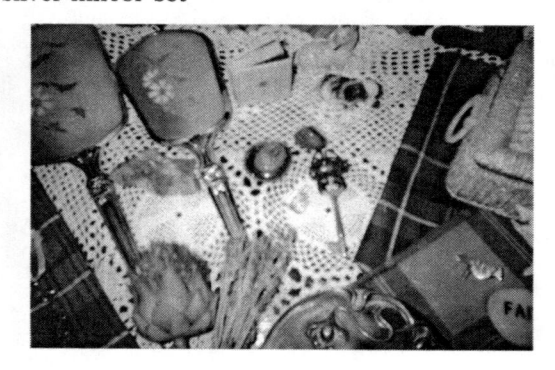

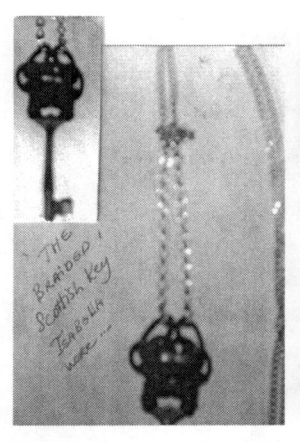

The braided Scottish 'key' Isabella wore and the doll house

The old fashioned purple/black hollyhock seeds given to me; my Mom and Dad planted them in their garden – so beautiful like velvet, *sweet dreams* pillow-case/with flowers embroidered on it (my mother made); in book, Nanny Belle makes it for Issy to remember the Flower Faeries!

The small willow and ash furniture I had given to me; in book Isabella's clan is known for making this furniture and a finally a quilt my mother made for me with Isabella in center of it; also small iron-on pictures of horse, butterflies and dragon fly by her name

The beautiful stallion mentioned in the book, a beautiful horse the author still loves till this day...

This is my son's dog spelt in real life, SANDI - mentioned in my two books! Sandi was a gentle loving soul/elemental who passed away suddenly and will always be missed!

This is a picture of HOWARD'S COVE on Prince Edward Island. This is where Isabella's clan in the book lived while on P.E.I. and where the real heart-shaped rock was found!

LAST BUT NOT LEAST the original Healing Faery Circle garden on P.E.I./not in the book per say but certainly this garden was made for *Isabella and the Healing Faeries*!

The circle was formed with FORGET-ME NOTS' and LILLY OF THE VALLEY however when they died down after I left the Island the family would plant some pansies in the circle to add color for the FAERIES! (**thank you!*) <u>Below</u>, the *author* in garden

95

'THE FOLLOWING PAGE is
current update for the AUTHOR'

Since book one, Isabella/The Secret of the Healing Faeries the author has moved to Perth, Ontario one hour outside of Ottawa, (Canada)! You will see a little bit more about this in ABOUT THE AUTHOR section at the back! Perth is a beautiful Scottish heritage town which is as pretty as it is loved by all those who live or come to visit there. On the following pages are some pictures of her recent adventures with her latest book launch and presentations with her Isabella books...

Book Launch at Eucalyptus Shop downtown Perth!

A beautiful little healing/holistic shop filled with wonderful crystal stones, inspiring books, CD'S, jewellery, lots of special soothing gifts for yourself or others and a helping 'faery faith' staff to help you! (*and Isabella books!*) *Thank you for the lovely newspaper article faery faith reporter!*

Author doing a presentation; a lovely successful book launch/selling *nine* books in *first* half hour! Next my display of my artifacts for book/book display and last my wonderful son and grandson bring me flowers from their garden to celebrate the occasion, (*My mom and husband sent flowers too THANK YOU!*)

99

ELMDALE SCHOOL COUNCIL (ESC)
Family, School and Community Working Together

Dear Parents/Guardians,
BOOKFEST IS ALMOST HERE!
A variety of guest speakers will visit most Elmdale classes next week as part of Bookfest's 'Authors in the Classroom' program. Thanks to

February 9, 2006

Author goes to annual book fest in Ottawa and just happens to know the 'young boy' xo who gave his school *my name* to do the presentation. On the coldest day in February the children presented me with a lovely SPRING plant! Had a great time!

The author was invited to present and talk about her Isabella book and journey with THE LANGUAGE EXPRESS team, parents and children celebrating their 10th year anniversary of their program! (A preschool speech and language program) The author wore her plaid apron and also got the children to sign, draw their hands and pictures about her visit there using their creative minds! (Lot's of cool drawings!)

The Author as you see likes to record her journey and share with others. Her book cover was framed and signed by all at first book launch, the Scottish napkins with (Scottish thistles) in Perth were signed by those who attended leaving lovely comments for the author, one of author's posters and book marks from book one and below a faery book was left for those to sign and leave emails for further updates!

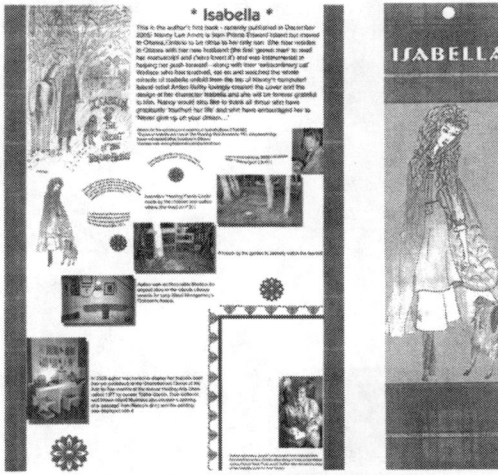

101

'Through this journey, the author herself has grown and changed through it all!'

The author, present day - to Isabella's beginning!

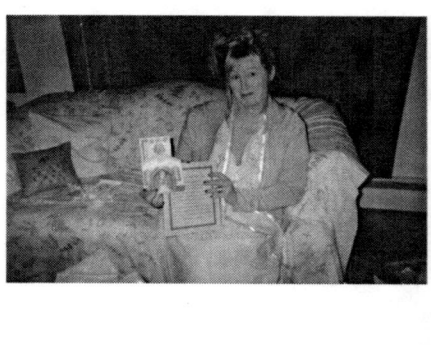

102

The 'AUTHOR'S SPECIAL SECTION' on *GARDENS*!
(Magical, mystical, soothing 'heaven on earth' gardens!)

'COME with me and let me share with you
The many FAERY GOOD sacred *secret* places
All about Faery circles and healing *spaces*
Starting with how and where and what to do...'

Starting with my good friend's picture of what she calls

"MY JACK IN THE BEAN STALKS!"

*Above <u>Morning Glories</u> that like to climb and these ones went up my friends steps, deck railing and <u>then</u> up her side of her house...amazingly beautiful in the wee' early hours of the day filling our *morning tea* with delight!

<u>On following pages</u>:
*Samples, sharing and 'real to goodness' *friends with permission* pictures and some of my own special garden pictures from my journal!

SAMPLE PICTURES OF

'ACTUAL 'FAERY' SPECIAL GARDENS'

*With SPECIAL Permission...

My mother's 'secret garden' of Forget-Me-Nots she made on the back of their property to remember her very own special mother! (There is also a path that winds down the hill to an extraordinary pond!)xo

Now what wonders did they bring back from their travels this time?
The Nome's garden of *secrets*? What fun! Their gardens are forever changing as gardens should and now Mom likes to do more watching as DAD putters - as she peers over with her 'watchful artist's eye'...xo

My Dad and Mom's special 'wildflower garden' they made one year - it was the most colorful *butterfly radiating* garden I have ever seen!

My sisters 'new' *creative garden* with pond and seat to ponder on with her 'loving gentle wisdom sister' ways (Two small *family members* reap the rewards of my sisters special place) xo

My *kindred spirit* friend's special cottage garden! She created this with pure love...and will have it *etched* in her memory as she moves on to greener pastures! (She knows the healing ways of 'hands in the dirt therapy as I') xo

'My family of 'faery faith friends' have container gardens and gardens with oriental flare, decks from heaven with 'plenty of chairs'...and many *memories* to cherish there!' xo (*That is me in the background filling my watering can...to water our famous 'faery circle garden' which is **secretly** hiding behind the small picket fence!)

Open this gate for a special surprise...peaceful, calm and things *silently* growing with love inside... xo

This property is lined with old trees, not just any old trees – magical, 'mystical faery faith trees'...how special is this for the *wee* folk... and my special 'faery faith friend' who saw many sightings and goings on with the elementals and many magical *moments*!

I love these big old trees (housing a home of *mushrooms* inside)... these are in Ontario but my *faery faith friend* who lived here is *now* back again in her homeland, the *healing shores* of P.E.I.! *(She is doing some *faery gardening* there but no updated pictures as yet!)xo

Ahhhhh this is my 'friend' with the GREEN thumb! (Whose name happens to start with ROSE which suits her to a 'T') xo When I moved from P.E.I. she lovingly took over my bird house and favorite garden chair knowing she would savor them like I did, as dear' friends!

Each year 'gardens change' and take over a new look – never the same – as with our lives we continually change, *forever growing* but remaining true to our natures!

And now the WINTER GARDEN...barren and still the *blanket of snow* covers and paints a new picture with promises of SPRINGTIME ahead...

This is indeed a *special magical* Faery Faith garden! One that grows <u>overnight</u> JUST after we have talked about MUSHROOMS being the homes for certain 'wee faery folk' just the day before! The Dad had just mowed the lawn the night before and 'lo and behold' overnight there appears a <u>RING OF MUSHROOMS</u>!!! Yes! So this precious little friend' of mine got a paper – made a sign and put rocks around <u>his </u>faery circle garden so no one would step on it! I happened to be a witness to it! (*And so did the rest of the family*...xo)

This is another precious garden 'made with love' – the summer of 06' while home on P.E.I. I made this *faery circle garden* with my niece and her friend using <u>16</u> <u>rocks </u>from their 'potato farm land' to form the circle – added a Faery statue in the middle and lavender! (16 adds up to Healing Faeries *favorite number* – **7**!) <u>One</u> <u>on right</u>: This is the original <u>Faery Circle Garden</u> I made on Prince Edward Island. It has 16 plants formed around its circle; Forget-me-nots and Lilly of the valley which will come up *every year*! This is springtime; this is truly a *sacred special place for me and all those who enter*!

111

This is my *friend* with the 'Jack of the Bean Stalk' Morning Glory plants which starts this section going...She also has a 'green and glorious' thumb and makes the *best cookies and tea ever*! Here she is with her sweet dog...she also grows some awesome kids! xo

Here are some 'corn flowers' by her fence...*she has a lovely garden* and like us all each year changes it around to please the *'eyes and pallet'!*

Two pictures/photographs from my cousin's (card making) creative business...I found these and had to put them in...she has an eye for beauty she captures with *her camera*...truly an *art* in motion! PINE is one of the favorite trees of Healing Faeries for healing properties and we all know the powerful remedies made from *oil* of sunflowers!

112

CREATING and *USING* your FAERY HEALING GARDENS!

'Get out into *NATURE*
where the *faeries roam and play*
create a safe haven - *coaxing them to stay!*'
By Nancy

Making Healing Faery Circles/Gardens

You may have a *healing faery (garden) or faery circle* in your garden already – or a garden you have created as a 'sanctuary' *for all who enter there*; a garden that brings a feeling of love, peace and hope to your soul!

When creating a Healing Faery Circle you can use perennials and herbs to form your circle, things that will come back again next year! Some of the plants we have used are; lily of the valley, forget-me-nots, crocus flowers, jumping jacks, violets and if you do not have plants or flowers we have used favorite rocks we have collected *forming the circle* (making sure the number of plants or rocks *add up* to the number SEVEN of course!) You could make one with all *lavender* plants, which would be pure 'heaven on earth' for the Healing Faeries harvesting some for yourself at *summers end*. The faeries *and* elementals also love water along with the birds and butterflies too! Entice the faeries with a small pond, fountain or even an old earthenware bowl full of water; a nice cool place for the faeries to stop and rest or do some *healing...*

Another thing you can do to coax the faeries to come to your garden is to *leave things* for them in the middle of your 'faery circle'! You can continually change it at *any time* when you get the *gentle nudge* from the faeries and your *FAERY SELF* to do so!

*Examples of things we have left in our circle: sea shells, dried herbs and flowers, little tiny objects of 'wee faery size' (like the children in my neighborhood where I used to live) ...little necklaces, colored stones, *colored sparkles* spread around the circle, little notes for the faeries and signs! We also had a 'faery tree' – where we hung plaid ties, ribbons and party streamers for birthdays and holidays! We even celebrated Isabella's birthday with candles, her picture and sparkles in the 'snow'!

**In our FAERY GARDEN on P.E.I. where I lived – *this summer* when home for holidays the family said the last of the streamers had just blown off this spring and had stayed on <u>for the THREE years</u> I have been away!

We also decorated our garden *for all seasons*; the faeries love *celebrations of any kind* and any added touches you come up with - they would *like*! We would dress up on Halloween Eve and Midsummer's Night Eve and dance around by candlelight or moonlight, sharing stories, leaving gifts, looking for other faery haunts; we would look for a grove of mushrooms on the property and we were *never* disappointed! (One of the parents even came and strung lights across the trees one year for us!) *The children continued the celebrations even after *I moved away*!

*(Share your STORIES or send PICTURES of your gardens to me!) Email me/if you need help ask your parents or guardians for help

EMAIL: <u>amos.nancy@yahoo.com</u>

'WINTER COMES TO FAERY GARDEN': Author sees the start of winters' *first snow* the morning after Halloween party in the faery garden! Our plaid ribbons are still 'blowing in the wind' on our SPECIAL FAERY TREE which we decorate for <u>all seasons</u>! (*Our *magical faery tree* <u>never</u> gets leaves and the faeries have asked *not to cut it down* and so far it stands – our bird feeder stands *full* ready for the season!)

Our *first snow* came early after our fun Halloween Eve party in our Faery Garden! What a surprise that was for all of us! The garden transformed overnight into a 'mystical magical white haven' for the faeries and all the elementals!

Snowed Halloween week!

The Faery Garden covered in a blanket of early snow....

Hi Nancy, — A NOTE from children's mom: we had a Halloween dress up party in the Faery Garden!

Thanks so much for the wonderful Haloween party — the boys (& girls) had a lot of fun — Thanks AND "It snowed overnight!!!" THE next day about

* Now we must prepare for our next big celebration! <u>Isabella's birthday</u> coming in *DECEMBER*! We must check our supplies...

The children start preparations by forming the Healing Faery Circle garden with *gold and blue sparkles* for Isabella's birthday which is on the 12th month, the 12th day the season being *winter*! *(DECEMBER 12th...) Then we decorate the circle for *ISABELLA*!

A closer look, a candle lit, a picture of Isabella adorned with purple ribbons and her *HEART SHAPED ROCK* from Howards' Cove! Lets' begin...

'ISABELLA'S BIRTHDAY MIRACLE!'

THAT DAY we made ISABELLA'S name with SPARKLES in the snow! <u>OVERNIGHT</u> we had got a fresh layer of fallen snow! The next morning I had a visitor! (*My dear friend who gave me the FAERY PIN that started this whole story going came for a visit!) We went down to the garden and I showed her where we had put Isabella's name by the 'wee faery castle' and I brushed away some snow and MIRACLE of FAERY miracles ICE had formed over the words – *ISABELLA*! We were able to brush all the snow away and there in ice was Isabella's name! I had to get the family to all come to witness this 'birthday miracle'! Our Faery Faith circle had <u>grown</u> that day (BELOW: <u>Birthday cards</u> for Isabella and I for our December birthdays mine is 7th, Issy's the 12th!)

119

My *faery faith sister* came to wish *us* Happy Birthday! She makes a wish in the circle! Below is Isabella's heart shaped rock and as you can see above you can still faintly see the sparkles under the snow forming the Healing Faery Circle! Below the children had tucked our 'wee' faery castle under the bushes to protect it from more snowfall – they had decorated it with small doll-like plastic balloons for the faeries and Isabella to enjoy! The neighbor's children and the two boys who lived below me continually left special things for the wee folk! What times we have had in that *sacred special* place!

Christmas is coming and the children and I made a sign to *WELCOME THE FAERIES* to the garden! As you can see we love to decorate for all seasons and all reasons! I am not sure if you can see the *small stars* blowing on our FAERY TREE! Below you can see the *path through our garden* is well worn! Again my dear sister who has come to visit me on Prince Edward Island holds a star we had in our garden to make yet *another wish...*

FINALLY SPRING AND SUMMER has come to our garden! AND with it a true Healing Faery miracle again!!!

Well earthen ware bowls are full of water, seashells decorate the paths near-by, two tree trunks act as tables and (sometimes seats) for the side of our garden but INSIDE the FAERY CIRCLE another as we call it FAERY faith garden MIRACLE has happened again! INSIDE the faery circle in the very MIDDLE *overnight* grew the most perfect mushroom. Not just an ordinary everyday mushroom but one of those STORYBOOK kinds - the brown with white spots you see in children's' books! YES! We all witnessed it and the secret and sacredness of it was, we all vowed we would NOT PICK IT but let it fall naturally as mushrooms will eventually do on their own! And once that happened about a week later my dear father (knowing the sacredness of it) lol photographed them for our memories and journal book! BELOW is the mushroom in the middle but on next page is a *closer picture*!

THE MIRACLE MUSHROOM that came to our garden that *perfectly* grew up in the very center of our Healing Faery Circle!

Do you suppose just maybe it was our sparkles we are forever *sprinkling* around our garden area or perhaps the FAEIRES were giving us back a 'gift' in our faery circle? Many times the children will leave wild flower bunches, seashells brought back from the beach or they leave small pieces of jewellery for the wee *girl faeries (from their dolls) They also have left small beautiful feathers, neat silver decorations, anything they think the faeries will like! Whatever it is – we will never forget!*

MIDSUMMERS NIGHT EVE has arrived! Let the celebrations begin!

Look at those faces, the streamers, the lights strung over the trees! Don't you just think the FAERIES and wee folk are delighting and celebrating with them tonight? To know to this day these children continue to celebrate Midsummer's Night Eve even though I have moved from Prince Edward Island! It makes my 'heart glad' and full of *LOVE* to have them as my *FAERY FAITH FRIENDS*! Our very first Midsummer's Night Eve we sang songs, I told stories of Isabella before she was even a published book, we lit candles and sat on blankets around the faery circle; we even took flashlights in hand to go on a faery haunt/mushroom hunt! We stayed out under the stars till we heard the parents go 'TIME TO COME IN' and oh it was *hard to come away* from that *fun!*

Creating
'YOUR OWN FAERY SPACE GARDEN'

*If you do not have a front or back yard!

(A WEE STORY INSIDE...)

NOTE FROM AUTHOR: You know I kept wondering Nancy; what are you doing 'going on about' what are you and Isabella trying to portray with the extra notes and extra pages? Well I have realized the FAERY IMPORTANT discovery of CREATIVITY and staying in the MOMENT. By staying in the NOW we are not thinking about future or past we are staying in the present and when we do this we are THERE to receive and there to SEE the 'miracles' as we have mentioned in this book! NOTHING is mundane in the NOW – nothing is too big for us to handle if we stay in the now...The flowers do smell more pretty, people smile more and I swear 'the sky more blue'...

But mainly we can turn NOTHING into beautiful something's in the now! As always I have an example...please stay with me in this moment! When I went home (to P.E.I.) for my first book launch a dear friend called to say she would see me on that day – she was quite excited to number one see me and two to tell me a <u>special story</u>!

> Well she took me aside and said, "Nancy, – remember when you lived on such and such street and had made the beautiful little garden behind your place? (right in 'heart' of downtown Charlottetown!) I said, "yes, I remember!" "WELL... a lady I know moved in there and was having a rough time and discovered YOUR GARDEN! She moved some overgrown tumbleweeds and there was a 'sacred secret garden' all for her JOY! It was as if a prayer was being answered; like a sign for her all would turn out well! My friend shed some wee tears as she shared this story with me – the lady wanted to come but was not up to it so asked my friend to please 'share the story' with me! Well we hugged and thought how beautiful a story is that! THIS IS WHAT I am talking about! It is the simple things in life we <u>MISS</u> if we are NOT staying in THIS MOMENT! Please, please as you bare with me through 'my little Isabella book' remember as we go through normal

days – there is NOTHING normal in our lives but everything if we LOOK closer and stay in the moment is like HEAVEN ON EARTH – <u>filled</u> with special miracles and special stories just like this one and the one to follow! We all have to start seeing the beauty and the miracles in our present day – in our simple <u>everyday lives</u> 'right in front of us begging for us to see!' (AND SHARE THEM - The Author)

THE AUTHORS OWN TRUE STORY:
(One you will love...)

No one knows better than the AUTHOR about small spaces for setting up your gardens when you do not have a good 'old' backyard! This is also a very SACRED wee STORY! This story takes place when I moved into a nine story *cement* apartment building in the west end of OTTAWA, Ontario! (*my first apartment with my new husband!)

When we moved to our sixth floor apartment they were working on our balconies (reconstructing the concrete). For that first summer no gardening was possible for me, not even 'container gardening'! I missed my old garden so much and the fun creating it each spring! So the very next year I started seeds inside with a passion! I had a 'lavish garden' started with container gardening – herbs and even tomatoes!

Well – I went home to P.E.I. for my very first *book launch* for Isabella/The Secret of the Healing Faeries, June 06' and had a friend look after it! It was a very early HOT HOT humid summer and to my dismay returned home with a dried out not much *living* garden! I must tell you I had a little 'faery cry' over it! So one weekend I was working and my husband's two teenage boys came for a visit! ALL that Saturday they worked day and into the night till I returned HOME – making me a *SECRET GARDEN* on our cement balcony! They made me 'close my eyes' and walk out to see it keeping it a SECRET! They had candles going, Celtic music playing and when I OPENED my eyes I was so SURPRISED! They had even put down a soft green outdoor carpet for me – filled the deck with potted plants, herbs, faery garden angels, a fountain and EVEN a pond on the end (hidden in a big Rubbermaid container) with SEVEN gold fish in it! I was for once - speechless!

I was so FAERY thankful and filled with gratitude that they did this for ME! My sixth floor garden was the talk of the building and as you can see a true FAERY FAITH MIRACLE and one filled with much love! I will never forget it ever! *THANK YOU* with all my heart! (*for all those who know me and know how much I love gardening you can appreciate this gift!) xo

*This picture was taken from our sixth floor apartment; overlooking a park, near a nice waterway! We had a lovely view from my new GARDEN PARADISE watching the Ottawa sunsets each night!

THIS is my garden – the top left is daytime and the bottom is a couple of nights after they TURNED my balcony into a *SACRED FAERY FAITH GARDEN*!

BELOW are just samples how my garden even though six floors up continually changed with chimes, herbs, tomatoes, Isabellas heart shaped rock, patio stones, more beautiful morning glories that lovingly stayed for most of the day and even my cats in *top right* picture got to enjoy the balcony with us! (*They are hiding in the shade of the wee willow and ash table!) xo

Author and family move to PERTH, Ontario!
New beginnings and another 'wee small space' for gardening!
(Nothing had ever been planted along this sidewalk area by our doors!)

*The author created a HEALING FAERY CIRCLE this time in this small space! She formed the circle with seven plants and seven bunches of rocks! She planted lavender, lemon balm, sage and thyme! Lined up containers on the wall and by summers' end you can see she once again planted her 'morning glories' she loves; again neighbors watched as this little postage stamp yard became a 'little haven' for her.

This is last but not least the remainder of sample pictures of SACRED places to meditate, relax and spin your dreams alive! A backyard deck two floors up, where beautiful elemental birds come to visit... a 'herb garden' in a bachelor pad I once had and a 'wonderful' veggie/SUNFLOWER garden my nephew and I made on their potato farm on P.E.I.! (His Mom and Dad said we could do whatever we wanted with that piece of land by the driveway! AND we did!) They are the tallest sunflowers I have ever personally grown and our pumpkins and squash and carrots were like they were made for giants...OKAY I know this book is about the 'wee' folk but I think perhaps we had some pretty WILD SEEDS there or was it the P.E.I. soil or the Island air? I am not sure but it sure makes you smile and perhaps will INSPIRE you to start creating a garden of some type SOON!

The Healing Faeries *SEVEN* favorite herbs/plants/oils and their healing properties:

LAVENDER
This is one of the Healing Faeries favorite herbs. The *smell* of lavender with its healing properties can quickly dissolve tension, stress, negativity and insomnia bringing a soothing calming effect on all who use it. Also used for bathing, for perfumes, to freshen up the linens and line in cupboards for a fresh scent! It is also used to relieve aches, pain and soothes sore tired muscles. *Can also be used in teas and foods for a pleasant unusual blend.

ROSEMARY
Rosemary is used in purification, cleansings, protection, sachets, enhancing love and at times used in BRIDAL wreaths promoting a long-lasting love and a long life ahead! It is a refreshing scent that is attractive to all - keeping one 'young at heart'! Also mixed in small amounts with breads and cheeses; when heated, it is at its maximum healing mode and has an exquisite taste!

THYME
This herb was used to bring strength and courage to all who use it and when the plant is wet with *dew* the scent itself can dispel anger, depression and soothe our dampened spirits!

LEMON BALM/VERBENA

Again this herb is used to uplift our spirits and helps clear negative thoughts that create patterns of ill health and despair. You can also use this herb in healing ointments for scrapes and bites.

PINE

Pine is used for clearing ones thoughts from negativity and replacing them with *joyful* thoughts. It also enables us to keep our memory 'crystal clear'. The smell of pine gives us hope and gives us the courage to move forward in our lives, especially on long winter nights; it makes us long for the renewal of life - of springtime!

JUNIPER

This plant helps to heal sores and wounds and if *sad* helps to find happiness again. Used for protection, sometimes the juniper berries were worn on a string as a necklace worn close to your heart or the juniper bush was grown close to the doorway, of your home!

FRANKINCENSE

This is one of the most sacred of oils used for purification and rituals. It can be used to purify houses, castles, sacred places like gardens, faery circles and also when burning the oil creates healing thoughts and creates a stance of unbelievable courage used for higher learning creating a more purposeful, meaningful life!

NOTE: When the Healing Faeries and Isabella gathered herbs...they were mixed and matched and blended for different 'healing remedies' that were *natural* to that day. By starting with these basic herbs and *believing* in the healing properties of the herbs – that was your 'key' for success as the *healer* and the *recipient*!

The Seven Favorite Healing Herbs/Plants/Oils

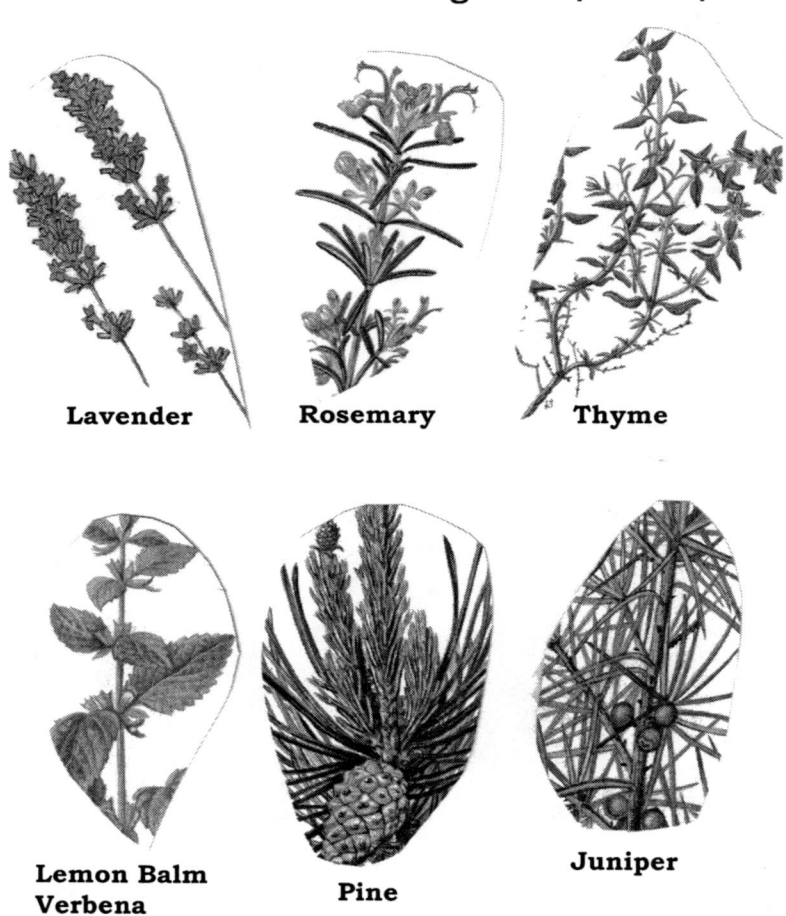

Lavender

Rosemary

Thyme

Lemon Balm Verbena

Pine

Juniper

Frankincense

The Healing Faeries *SEVEN* favorite Healing Stones and their healing properties:

AMETHYST
This purple stone promotes *healing* to all who wear or hold it in their hands. It relieves stress and transforms negative energy into positive energy. It is one of the most powerful and healing stones healing body, mind and spirit! It brings about immediate feelings of love, peace and tranquility! This is the most important healing *stone* for the Healing Faeries and one they use often.

AMBER
This is a very energizing stone of the pine trees! *PINE* is also a very healing tree of the Healing Faeries. The smell of pine alone invigorates and bestows renewed energy and stamina; it gives one hope. The stone or solidified sap of a pine tree with its golden hue has ancient powers giving us strength, wisdom, with a calming soothing effect. It softens and purifies our heart and spirit and draws out negativity.

AVENTURINE
This is a stone that promotes creativity, allowing one to follow their intuition, feelings and thoughts. Green Aventurine makes us see opportunities in all our situations leading us to the abundance of the earth. It promotes healing and growth leading us to our full potential.

CITRINE
This golden stone gives us a renewed zest for living! It helps us to seek the truth, baths us in protection and brings us generous *abundance* in life. Its color soothes

us and gives us strength to move forward in our lives. The sunshine hue can also surround not only ourselves but we can visualize it going out surrounding our home, our loved ones and out into the entire earth with its healing power.

JADE
Jade stands for peace and wisdom and helps us to balance matters of the *heart* with *matters* of the world. Also the Jade stone helps us to balance nature following the laws of the land and laws of the elementals who live on it. In times of trouble Jade acts as a healing influence and helps to dissipate angry situations.

CLEAR CRYSTAL QUARTZ
This stone is one of the most highly evolved stones of the gemstone family. It helps bring clarity, healing, transformation and awakening. It is a stone to help purify our thoughts and our hearts. It helps us to be more positive allowing us to move forward and bring our hopes, dreams and wishes into reality. The energy of the stone vibrates love, harmony and peace to all who wear or use this stone. It also aids in sending out - healing positive thoughts and *energy* to all peoples, animals and the earth itself!

ROSE QUARTZ
This is called the stone of *love*. It creates all sorts of love connections, self-love, healing love, caring and compassion, motherly love, friendship and long-lasting love! It creates healing nurturing and comfort for all who wear or use this stone! It can attract loving people into your life and helps you to be more loving to others, animals and the earth itself!

NOTE:
Although there are lots more healing stones - these were just the seven favorite used by Isabella and the Healing Faeries! *Seven* was their favorite number and at times they would use *combinations* of numbers adding to seven. For example, in larger faery circle gardens they would plant 16 plants to form the circle adding up to the number *seven*!

*I do not have any pictures for the stones but perhaps one day you can get to a shop that sells *crystal stones* and see them for your *elf-self*!
(and *possibly* collect some...)

INTRODUCTION...

'For all those who have not read my first book this section has been dedicated to a famous author! You will recognize her name as soon as you hear it...what you may not know is I was born in Ontario and left as a 'wee child' moving to the Maritimes but ended up spending most of my life on the beautiful shores of Prince Edward Island! And for 'changing tides and family ties' I am now back in Ontario...'

"As in my book like Isabella and like Lucy Maud, I too have left my heart there!"

"DEAR Peoplefolk the following pages are for the children to understand HOW a story gets started – what makes someone 'want to write', what inspires them and please, please encourage all children and adults alike to create, create, create and never give up on their dreams!"

The following pages are dedicated to one of the authors' <u>favorite authors</u>, LUCY MAUD MONTGOMERY! To follow an authors' journey and to get to know him or her, you have to do *research*! Lucy Maud has been one of my mentors – which means, *teacher, wise speaker, advisor, someone you look up to and admire*! If you have not read any background on Lucy Maud the famous author of Anne of Green Gables, (my) most favorite book she has written about her life is <u>The Alpine Path</u>! With today's access on the internet you can look her up and see with your own eyes, her background, her history, even down to her *personal* journals and *scrapbooks* she kept of her journey! She too had an adamant love for nature, the elementals and the *wee faeries* which she mentions in passages in her books!

*Note: (The author entered her <u>original story of Isabella</u> in The Islands Literary awards on Prince Edward Island...She won an Honorable Mention for her story in the Lucy Maud Montgomery's children's awards division which gave her the courage to KEEP GOING!) Like Lucy Maud, Nancy has found it takes a 'lot of courage' to keep going and to keep your <u>dream alive</u>!

LUCY MAUD MONTGOMERY

(Born: Clifton, Prince Edward Island - November 30th, 1874)
(Died: Toronto, Ontario - April 24th, 1942)

'Children and adults alike all know about the famous author of <u>Anne of Green Gables</u>... The following pages are a *dedication* to the author's memory!'

Dear Children and the *child* in each one of us:

This is to remind us of the <u>*woman*</u> who made up the lovely character and stories of *ANNE*! In the true spirit of the Island way Lucy Maud Montgomery shows us the importance of keeping in touch with the *Kindred Spirits* in our lives by staying in touch with our 'friends and loved ones'!

LUCY MAUD never gave up on her dreams and her love for Prince Edward Island never dwindled even though she left the place of her birth! She kept the ISLAND *SPIRIT* alive through her books and through 'her spirit'- she still to this day encourages us to *open* up our imaginations and those who have the 'urge to write', to do so!

This POEM is DEDICATED to the MEMORY OF:
LUCY MAUD MONTGOMERY

FORGET ME NOT

Cherished
Dreams
Have transpired
For in my heart
I've planted seeds
Of Lilac trees
And Matrimony
Forget-Me-Nots
And Lilly
Of the Valley
A sacred spot
Of Daffodils'
A stretch of land
And rolling hills
The ocean breathes
Her gentle mists
As daylight fades
The night persists
The stars do form
A wondrous sight
For up above
Hangs Little Dipper
Spraying thoughts
Just like the dew
Forget-me-not
My Lady Slipper

By Nancy

In all of Lucy Maud's writings, scrapbooks and passages she brings about the importance of the 'simple beautiful things' of life! Not the 'material' side or the mundane! Her imagination takes you on a *journey* that lasts and lasts and brings about a 'peace' not all authors can give you!

Lucy Maud's birthplace in Clifton, Prince Edward Island

In this picture Nancy stands in front of the Author Lucy Maud's home the Leaskdale Manse in Leaskdale, Ontario. (This is where Lucy Maud moved after she married and left Prince Edward Island)

*They say `HOME IS WHERE YOUR HEART IS' which is true but I also BELIEVE that your <u>faery faith sense</u> of *HOME* always stays *WITHIN* you no matter where you go! You just have to 'close your eyes' and there it is - your memories, smells and feelings that can *bring you instantly back 'home'!*

Isabella lived on the healing shores of Prince Edward Island and fell in love' with the red soil, the ocean and the Island way, the *peoplefolk* way of life! When she left the Island to return to Scotland she not only took with her the 'grace' of the land but also took with her some of her favorite things; one of which was a 'heart-shaped' rock from Howard's Cove! Even though she had to leave she will never forget Prince Edward Island and what she had learnt there! In the story it says Prince Edward Island is where she found *healing* and *much love* and it is here that she shall leave her 'heart'!

Lucy Maud left Prince Edward Island but took with her the memories of her life's journey and left us a 'legacy of her life' through her journals and pictures in her scrapbooks! On the *wave* of these gifts and her *love* of Prince Edward Island the author continued to write *several* more books in Ontario! Lucy Maud also went to Scotland on her honeymoon and I am sure *returning* with a feeling of renewed strength, energy and *spirit* looking forward to her new life ahead! With this change she was able to share more of her life, stories and invigorate us with her words!

"No matter *where we go*, whatever *life brings us* - it's the 'journey' and all our experiences that make us *who we are*! Each one of us has so much to offer and to share with one another! The Healing Faeries believe that anything is possible – only if you *TRULY* believe!

It's up to us to share this journey with our children so let's give our children a 'piece of their history' and let *them* <u>continue the story</u>"...

Nancy has just worked on a FAMILY *JOURNAL* BOOK, a *keepsake for her son* – it has taken almost a whole year to do – but it was worth it! She also made it in 'such a way' he can pass it on to his son!

Quote from Lucy Maud Montgomery:
(From the book, The Alpine Path)

'I had, in my vivid imagination, a passport to the geography of Fairyland. In a twinkling I could – and did – whisk myself into regions of wonderful adventures,
unhampered by any restrictions of time or place.'

ABOVE: Nancy on the shores of Prince Edward Island saying 'goodbye' shortly before she moved to Ontario.

*THIS POEM IS DEDICATED TO:
'Our *FAVORITE PLACES* we have lived'...By Nancy

MY SPECIAL PLACE

My first love
I thought I'd
Shared
Was a person long ago
But this strange feeling
Deep inside
Is for a *house*
I used to know
The memory
Keeps haunting me
I close my eyes
And visualize
The way things
Used to be
The house, the fields
The apple tree
The view upon the hill
It pulls and tugs
My heartstrings so
Like an old tune
I should know

Nancy's favorite, *the CHURCHILL HOUSE*,
Churchill, Prince Edward Island

TWO POEMS for ISABELLA

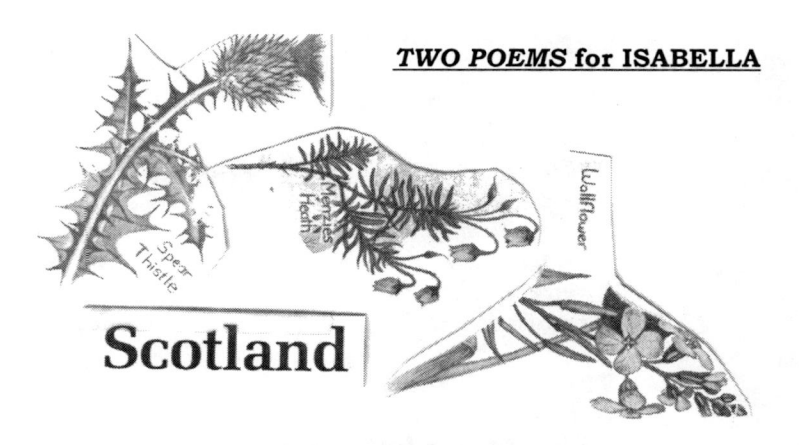

Scotland

'While on Prince Edward Island Isabella often thought of Scotland, she missed the moors, the misty rugged coast and her favorite flower, the Scottish Thistle! Isabella never dreamt she would love Prince Edward Island so much and when she returned to her homeland she found she missed the red earth, the flowers, and her favorite 'Feathered Friends', the Blue Jays – their color matching the blue Scottish plaid tartan she wore!' *Poems on following page...*

THE SCOTTISH THISTLE

The Purple Thistle
Stands up tall
Upon her leaves
The dewdrops fall
Up to the sky
One has to look
To see the view
She offers you

The rugged coast
Sends off her mist
As if a *tender loving kiss*
The rains may come
The winds may blow
But stands the *thistle*
Brave and tall
Brilliant purple
Stretches forth
To meet the mornings' glow

BLUE JAYS

On winter mornings
Just past dawn
Across the porch
Across the lawn
Stands just a tall
And single tree
Upon its branches
Lined in blue
Are several Blue Jays
Calling me…

They watch me close
For we're old friends
As I gather food for them
They wait until I'm back inside
And then they make that *famous cry*
With bellies full, my friends depart
Until tomorrow my dear hearts…

For those who have NOT read MY FIRST BOOK

**The MEANING OF THE WORDS for
THE HEALING FAERIES!**

T   -   THOUGHTS
H   -   HEAL
E   -   EVERYONE

H   -   HELP
E   -   EVERYONE
A   -   ALWAYS
L   -   LIVE
I   -   IN the
N   -   NOW
G   -   GRACEFULLY and with GRATITUDE

F   -   FAITH
A   -   ALWAYS
E   -   ETERNALLY
R   -   REIGNS
I   -   IN
E   -   EVERY
S   -   SUNRISE

ABOUT THE AUTHOR

Nancy Lee Amos lived on the *healing* shores of Prince Edward Island for over 'half her life' – to Nancy it is her *HOME*! In May 2003 she moved to Ottawa, Ontario to be closer to her son and only child and in doing so her life has indeed changed! She remarried in 2005, published her first children's book and in 2006 became a *grandmother*! Not only has her family grown but also her character *Isabella*; since then Nancy has finished Book II and is working on her third and final in her *Isabella series*!

Nancy's interest in children and the 'healing aspect of life' has lead her to create Isabella and the Healing Faeries to help give children and adults *alike* 'hope' and in turn the *faery faith* needed in order to make their *dreams* come true! Nancy has worked with children for most of her life – in the past in a Treatment Foster Care Program and in her recent past as a Nanny for several small children. The one thing Nancy has discovered is it's the 'simple things in life' that *heal us* and the universal need to find *peace and happiness* that binds us all! In the first book, Isabella/The Secret of the Healing Faeries you are introduced into the life of Isabella who had to do some healing of her own in order to *grow* and be able to help others! It was her chosen destiny! In Book II, Isabella/Reunites the Healing Faeries Isabella is now able to 'break free' from her past and discover who she truly is and goes on to lead her people showing them new ways to follow their dreams as well as her own!

Nancy has also won an Honorable Mention for her original story of her character, Isabella in the Island Literary Awards for the Lucy Maud Montgomery Children's award. She also had her story on display at the Confederation Center of the Arts in Charlottetown, P.E.I. in the annual Healing Art Show conducted by curator, Trisha Clarkin. The author had her first *successful* book launch at the Reading Well Bookstore on P.E.I. June, 2006 - has taken her work to schools and donated copies of her book to school libraries in Charlottetown, P.E.I., New Brunswick, Ottawa and Perth! Nancy has more book launches scheduled for this fall. Nancy has sold copies of her first book all across Canada, as far as Hawaii and the UK!

UPDATE: Nancy presently resides in beautiful Perth, Ontario which surprisingly enough is named after PERTH in Scotland! (See www.beautifulperth.com) The town is a beautiful heritage town almost one hour from Ottawa, which is also the present home of her son. Nancy has since had a wonderful successful book launch for her first book in Perth at the (Eucalyptus Shop) introducing people to Isabella and the Healing Faeries. Also on this note for all those who have waited so *patiently* for her second book; with apology for the delay *but* coming from the belief that everything we will ever need is in THIS present MOMENT - there is no time like the NOW to bring Isabella II to you with love, gratitude, healing, light and great universal thoughts of togetherness for our 'heavenly life on earth!'

A new WEBSITE is currently being made for Isabella and author to check go to:

http://www.51875.authorworld.com

****

&&&&&&&&&&&&&&&&&&&&&&&&&&&&&&&&&&&&&&

&&&&&&&&&&&&&&&&&&&&&&&&&&&&&&&&&&&&&&

****

The author's books are *dedicated* to the children she has worked with and to the *memory* of her grand-dog Sandi whose name is mentioned in her two books! In collage style above is the author, her husband William – (who appeared *after* the *William* in her book!), the *famous pose* standing on a 'stool' for her wedding *kiss*, the couple on Prince Edward Island June 06' and their two cats Wallace and *wee* Bella!

156

THE FAERIES BELIEVE: In giving **THANKS**, being <u>thankful</u> and sharing their 'gifts' with others...

- MY THANK YOU -

'I know the *wee ones* won't understand some of my book just yet – *but they will* – and we can show them the *importance* of saying THANK YOU <u>while we still can</u>'...

On the following pages are just a few of the special people who have touched my life! **NOW'S** *the time to tell those* special people just how much they mean to me! Please help teach our children h*ow* to be *thankful* for <u>'everything and everyone'</u> in their lives!

Love and Sparkles...Nancy and Isabella!
(PEOPLE ARE GIFTS!)

****

I wish to THANK...

My Mom and Dad, my husband and his boys, my son and his family, my sisters and brother and their children, all my grandparents who have passed on...To all my 'Aunties & Uncles', cousins and all their families! You have given me the 'pattern and the scissors' and let me go! But it's the connection – the weaving of ALL OF OUR LIVES TOGETHER that has made me who I am today! THANK you for believing in me and my dream!

*While I am talking about (family and friends) I would like to share another important thing I have learnt through Isabella and the Healing Faeries - about the <u>VOICES</u> and <u>SCENTS</u> of our loved ones! They are a very important part of our lives...to hear a familiar voice is like water to a flower and the smell of Auntie Nancy's vanilla musk perfume is like a hug itself – my nieces and nephews and children who I have worked with and have not seen for years have told me – you still 'smell the same' – I remember that smell when we got in your car! I know the smell of my Mom and Dads home...and I still remember my grandmothers! There is no bottling of this, no way to capture this - except to 'pass on the importance of it to our children!' *Nanny Belle's rosemary oil, Isabella's fathers voice...my grandsons' baby powder smell, the way he turned his head <u>at one month old</u> to hear his fathers' voice and now his 'wee' voice that says Nana, 'I lov ew!' at nineteen months!

To all my 'friends' on Prince Edward Island; C.M., R.G., V.F., M.D., A.C., D.H., K.K., R.W., U.S., M.C., W.E., T.C., S.M., E.G., B. &S.K., and all their mates! To ALL the CHURCHILL gang! My new friends in Ottawa and now Perth who took me under their wings! You are KEEPERS! My faery faith friends! There are many more! (*And many more who are not with us anymore but are in our <u>hearts</u>!) They know who they are!

To my ex-supervisor T.K., my co-workers and all the children I worked with! To all my Nanny families and their children – you know who you are! I have pictures and 'gifts' and memories I will cherish 'forever'! Thank you for all your love, support, inspiration and most of all – <u>believing in Isabella and myself</u>!

CONTINUED:

I wish to THANK YOU for your INSPIRATION...

Certain musicians have inspired me on my journey, <u>our own Island musicians</u>: my dear friend, Richard Wood with his CELTIC touch! Although he has been busy traveling the world spreading his 'fiddle fever', he's never too tired to stop and say 'hello' to us or share a tale of Scotland or abroad; even playing a tune or two for dear friends! (My favorite CD that <u>still keeps me going today</u> is FIRE DANCE!)

Our Lennie Gallant with his Island rustic songs, favorite CD OPEN WINDOW – all the talented musicians who used to play at the open mikes, their host who gave them support and encouragement along with drawing the crowd of 'locals' including myself' during those long P.E.I. winters...Dave Howard, Favorite song: LEGACY!

Loreena McKennitt was my 'female inspiration'! Listening to her haunting mystical ballads while I wrote my books helped me to create and shape my character Isabella and actually getting to see Loreena perform in Charlottetown, with her harp, the stage full of candelabra's 'all aglow' wearing a velvet dress visualized how I saw my character Isabella! My favorite CD THE VISIT!

My faery faith friend Valerie Farqharson for all her 'heartfelt' priceless information on all her courses she has taken and shared with me about the healing ways – Reiki, Reflexology, the Healing Stones, Therapeutic Touch, the Native teachings she learnt from great teachers and friends! And for the FAERY PIN she gave me to put on my apron that started my whole ISABELLA journey going...Thank YOU!

My HERO and favorite author – Lucy Maud Montgomery! My favorite book, the ALPINE PATH! She also loved the faeries and has mentioned them in passages you find in the book – The Spirit of Place! YES I loved ANNE of Green Gables too; my favorite ANNE was Megan Fellows who to this day is an amazing actress! My favorite Island author – David Weale, he can spin a tale' with a 'voice' you can listen to for hours!

Thank you to Peter at the Buzz newspaper and my Dad for getting article to Guardian on their request, Angela for my great interview with CBC radio, John and Sue from the Reading Well bookstore; wonderful hosts and wonderful book

launch, Churchill Pub staff, Jeff/Merriam Print, all those who came for book launch debut! Also a 'special thanks' to my illustrator, Island artist Arden Belfry who designed my Isabella 'perfectly' and designed both covers. Thank you to all those in <u>Perth</u> who welcomed me with OPEN ARMS and helped with the book launch at Eucalyptus Shop – you are true healing faeries and my present boss/faery faith friend for her <u>ever</u> continued support!   And for now...my dear representative from my publishing company – there are no words to express your expertise and support from day one – THANK YOU Jennifer! Thank you <u>all</u> who bought your books!
*Love and Sparkles, Nancy and Isabella!

'ISABELLA, QUEEN of THE HEALING FAERIES'

'Isabella says THANK YOU for believing in the Healing Faeries and for sharing your time with her! Till the next book she shall watch over you – you will know when she is near, you may find an unexpected <u>sparkle</u> on your shirt or on the table or the floor - another sign the faeries are near; also her favorite times are early morn and early eve and in the 'quiet times' of your heavenly day...

*******NOTES FOR FAERY FAITH FRIENDS*******

SPECIAL LIST OF BIRTHDAYS OF FAERY FAITH FRIENDS

JANUARY

FEBRUARY

MARCH

APRIL

MAY

JUNE

JULY

AUGUST

SEPTEMBER

OCTOBER

NOVEMBER

DECEMBER

May all your dreams come true...
HAPPY BIRTHDAY to YOU!

(A birthday cake my sister gave to ME!)

*******FAERY SIGHTINGS AND SPECIAL MAGICAL MOMENTS*******

DATE:

NOTES:

DATE:

NOTES:

DATE:

NOTES:

DATE:

NOTES:

DATE:

NOTES:

DATE:

NOTES:

DATE:

NOTES:

*YOU HAVE TO BELIEVE in the magic of the NOW...
till we meet again...*

**EVERYTHING YOU WILL EVER WANT OR NEED
IS RIGHT HERE RIGHT NOW**

Nancy and Isabella